HAPPY Birthd
CARa KAY TINGLEY
July 3rd, 1986
Nicole Sager

Once Upon a Friendship

by Jane Sorenson

STANDARD PUBLISHING
Cincinnati, Ohio   2982

Library of Congress Cataloging in Publication Data

Sorenson, Jane.
  Once upon a friendship.

  (A Jennifer book ; 6)
  Summary: As their friendship deepens, Jennifer
and Heidi make important discoveries about physical
attractiveness and inner beauty.
  [1. Beauty, Personal—Fiction. 2. Friendship—
Fiction. 3. Christian life—Fiction] I. Title.
II. Series: Sorenson, Jane. Jennifer book ; 6.
PZ7.S7214n 1985   [Fic]   85-2600
ISBN 0-87239-932-X

To Mary McDonald
... always my sister
... always my friend

Chapter 1

Grandma in for a Landing

Lord, it's me, Jennifer.

I couldn't believe it. I was about to go over a waterfall. Both Mack and Matthew Harrington were swimming to save me. Which one would reach me first? Or would I be dashed on the rocks below?

I opened my eyes. Naturally, it was just a dream. I realized that I had forgotten to pull out the button on my alarm clock. And, in the bathroom next door, the shower was already running full blast.

I squinted at the clock. Eight-thirty. And Grandma's plane was due at eleven-thirty. I'd have to get moving. Unfortunately, I couldn't go far until I got a turn in the bathroom.

Light peeked around the edges of the window shades. It wasn't sunny. Since nobody could see me anyhow, I raised each of the three shades halfway up. Mom says uneven shades give people driving past a bad impression. Lord, do You agree?

As soon as the water stopped, I grabbed my robe and stood outside the bathroom door. I wasn't taking any chances on my other brother getting in ahead of me.

While I waited, I heard the whirring of a hair dryer. *My* hair dryer!

"Blow it in your room!" I yelled.

Nothing happened.

I pounded on the door. "Dry your hair in your room!" I yelled again. Still nothing happened. Nothing, that is, in the bathroom. At the other end of the hall, Pete stuck his head out of his room. "Quiet!" he yelled.

Behind me, my parent's door opened. Dad stood there in his bare feet looking like a full-size version of Justin— hair going every direction and a hand clutching his pajama bottoms. "Just what," he asked softly, "is going on out here?"

"I'm sorry," I said. "I was just trying to get into the bathroom."

"Next time try more quietly," Dad said. His door closed. That's easy for him to say. He doesn't have to share a bathroom with two boys.

"Hi, Jennifer," my younger brother said. "Are you as hyper as I am?"

Well, there I stood, all ready to let Justin have it for

hogging the bathroom. But I just couldn't, that's all. "For sure," I smiled.

This is Grandma Green's first visit to Philadelphia. As You know, she has to come alone, since Grandpa Green is now in Heaven with You.

By the time I finished my shower, I remembered that Pete was still waiting. I unplugged the hair dryer and took it to my room.

Figuring out what to wear to the airport wasn't easy. I couldn't decide if jeans were appropriate or not. Although I knew Grandma wouldn't care, I wasn't so sure about Mom. I decided to chance it. I put on jeans and my pink sweater. If it turned out to be cold, I'd wear my down vest on top.

My hair is nearly stick-straight now that it's longer again. When I had it styled last spring, it got sort of wavy. Figuring out the styles here hasn't been easy. I don't know if Illinois is ahead of Philadelphia or behind!

Just as I was about ready to go downstairs, I looked in the mirror. Oh, no! Right on the end of my nose was a large, red bump! I touched it. It hurt! I couldn't believe it. I'd be spending at least the weekend looking like Rudolph the Red-nosed Reindeer. Lord, no offense, but did Jesus ever get a pimple?

Mom was waiting in the kitchen. From the way the table was set, I guessed we were all going to eat together. Usually our breakfast is straggly.

"Good morning," Mom smiled.

"Hi," I said. "What's for breakfast?"

"Are the others coming?"

"I think so. When do we have to leave for the airport?" I asked.

"We're aiming for ten. It's more fun to be at the gate when someone arrives."

"Especially Grandma," I said. "Are you nervous?"

"Why should I be nervous?" Mom looked puzzled.

"Women are always nervous when their husband's mother is coming," I told her. "Laurie's mom always cleans out every cabinet."

"It depends on the mother," Mom said. "Actually, I'd probably be more nervous if *my* mother were coming!"

"Thanks for last night," I said. At our meeting to plan the next youth-group social, Mom offered to help us with a spaghetti supper. "The kids are really excited about having it here."

"That's what a home is for," Mom said. Then she added, "Mack Harrington didn't seem in any hurry to leave."

"You noticed," I said. I could feel this huge smile filling up my whole face. It was so embarrassing. "He's super!" I added.

"That seems to be a common Harrington trait," Mom said. "I thought Matthew was pretty nice too."

"Right," I said.

"When I was in college," Mom said, "we had a rule that we didn't date two guys in the same fraternity at once."

"What's a fraternity?" I asked.

"Like a club for guys in college. They call each other 'brothers.'"

"Why did you have that rule?"

"Can't you guess?"

"So they wouldn't get jealous?" I guessed right. "But the Harringtons are real brothers. They wouldn't get jealous."

Mom just looked at me. She didn't say anything more.

In spite of the morning hassle, everyone came to breakfast in a good mood. As You know, we never have pancakes and sausage on an ordinary Saturday morning. This day was special.

"Shall I wear Pops' fishing hat?" Pete asked. When our grandfather died, my brother inherited it. Because we all loved Pops so much, it is a very special hat.

"Let's leave it here," Dad said. "It might make Grandma feel bad if she saw it when she wasn't expecting it." The rest of us agreed.

The drive from our house to the airport is tricky, but Dad made it without getting lost or asking directions. And we found a great spot in the parking garage on level two. It still seems funny to go to an airport that isn't wall-to-wall crowded like Chicago's O'Hare.

Actually, there were quite a few people meeting Grandma's flight. We watched through the huge window while the plane landed and taxied over to our gate. Dad told Pete, Justin, and me it was OK to stand closer to the door.

The plane must have been full. A whole lot of people

came through. Most weren't smiling. Some glanced around anxiously. Others with briefcases walked swiftly, as if they had done this a hundred times before.

"There she is!" Justin hollered.

"Grandma!" Pete yelled. "We're over here!"

Although she looked very much alone, she was smiling her darling little smile that wrinkles the corners of her eyes. "Oh, my goodness!" she said. "You're all here to meet me! Wonderful!"

We nearly caused a traffic jam because we all wanted to hug her—even Mom and Dad. The other people were all grinning at us.

"She must be somebody special," said a man standing nearby.

"Correct," Justin said.

"Somebody very excellent," I added. Then it was my turn for a hug. We nearly squished each other. As You probably noticed.

Chapter 2

Off-Season Tourists

Lord, it's me, Jennifer.

As You know, Grandma Green almost bounced along the red carpet on the way to picking up her luggage. She could have flown in without a plane.

"Mom, I suppose it's ridiculous to ask," Dad said, "but are you tired?"

Grandma grinned. "You're right," she said. "It *is* ridiculous to ask."

"She'll probably crash later," Pete told me. It is hard to talk when you're almost running in an airport. I nodded my head. I certainly didn't want to hurt Grandma's feelings.

"Do you have your baggage stubs?" Dad asked.

Grandma fished in her purse. She zipped one compartment open, closed it, then tried another. "I like lots of compartments," she explained. "But in a new purse, it's hard to remember which is which." Fortunately, she finally produced the tickets.

"How many?" Pete asked. "And what do they look like?" He and Justin would get the suitcases.

"Two," Grandma said. "Brown with tan trim. A garment bag and a Pullman."

"They look brand new," Mom observed.

"I just bought them," Grandma said, as we stashed them in the back of the station wagon.

"You got new luggage just to visit us?" I asked.

"Partly," Grandma said. "Did you realize I never was on a plane before the funeral?"

"I guess I didn't know that," Dad said.

"Jay and I always drove to Florida so we'd have our car. And after we moved down there, he never really wanted to go anywhere else," Grandma explained. "To be honest, there are a lot of places I'd like to see!"

"Grandma Green, World Traveler," I said. "Sounds good!"

"My luggage has real leather trim," Grandma said. "At first I thought at my age it was silly to spend so much. But then I realized I could live twenty or thirty more years! No use being stuck with cheap luggage. That leather trim is my commitment to living a long life!"

"Mom, you're the greatest!" Dad said. He curved the car around the ramp leading to the street.

12

"Are you hungry?" Mom asked.

As a matter of fact, Grandma is always hungry. Lord, do You know how she can eat so much and stay so little?

"How about if we drive into the city to show Grandma the sights? And would anyone like a hoagie?" Dad asked.

We all cheered, even Grandma. I was pretty sure she had no idea that a hoagie is a special Philadelphia sandwich. After the hoagies, naturally we had to get ice cream and milk shakes on Spruce Street.

To be honest, the historical district looks really gloomy at this time of year. But Grandma thought everything was *wonderful*. She even got tears in her eyes when she touched the Liberty Bell. I couldn't believe it. Because of the season, we didn't have to stand in line at Independence Hall. She read every historical sign we passed.

"It's wonderful," she kept saying. "To think that I've actually seen the first hospital in the United States."

Betsy Ross' house was *wonderful* because it was so narrow! Well, of course, there was the flag thing too. And Ben Franklin was pronounced a "rascal" right in his printing shop.

Frankly, it is embarrassing to admit it, but Grandma knows more about Philadelphia's history than we do! She asked Mom if she had considered buying a town house in Society Hill. Mom hadn't.

"Valley Forge is on the way home," Dad said, finally.

"Oh, Peter," Grandma said, "what a thrill that will be!"

I wasn't so sure. It looks pretty bleak at this time of

year. In the spring, the dogwood trees are in bloom, and everything is beautiful. And in the early fall, people drive miles to see the dogwoods' red leaves and berries. Now there's really nothing.

Pete and Justin didn't even quarrel while we drove the Schuylkill Expressway. I don't think it even occurred to them. Grandma entertained us with a detailed description of her flight. She nearly got locked in the bathroom!

But Grandma didn't say a word as we drove into Valley Forge Park. Dad made a few of his typical "tour guide" comments. When we passed the soldiers' huts, Grandma asked him to stop the car. She got out and marched over to read the sign. My brothers followed her. Dad, Mom, and I stayed in the car.

"Imagine!" was all she said.

Washington's Headquarters was closed. Mom was disappointed, but Grandma just marched over, peered in windows she could reach, and examined the outside of other buildings nearby.

"Ready to go?" Dad asked when she got back into the car.

"That other trail," Grandma said. "I'd like to take that."

"But it doesn't really lead anywhere," Dad explained.

Grandma didn't answer. Dad started driving. It was the bleakest spot I think I've ever seen.

"Stop the car, Peter," Grandma said. "Everybody out!"

We looked at each other. But naturally we obeyed.

14

Everybody obeys Grandma. Justin rolled his eyes when she wasn't looking.

"Feel that breeze," Grandma said. "It could get pretty cold here in the winter, couldn't it?"

"Right," said Pete. Personally, I was glad I had worn my down vest.

"More than 3,000 soldiers died here," Grandma said.

I knew there hadn't been a battle. I made that mistake in the spring. "How?" I asked.

"Hunger. Sickness. Cold." Grandma looked around the area. "Washington had 11,000 men here the winter of 1777 to 1778. Their only shelter was those little huts like we saw back there. They had no uniforms—hardly any warm clothing, not even shoes, and little to eat."

"Why didn't the British capture them?" Pete asked.

"They were partying in Philadelphia," Grandma said. "They didn't want to come out here in the cold to fight."

"It must have been pretty discouraging," Dad said. "Couldn't the Americans get food from the countryside?"

"The farmers didn't want to give them supplies because they couldn't pay for them," Grandma explained.

"How selfish," Justin said.

"That's easy for you to say," I said. "It wasn't your stuff."

"Our independence was won partly at this place," Grandma said. "Just through loyalty to George Washington and the cause of freedom."

"Through survival," Dad said.

Gradually, we all got back in the car. Nobody said anything as we rode through the bleak trails. I could just picture those cold and hungry men huddled around campfires.

"Grandma, I think this is the best time of year to see Valley Forge after all," I said.

"How do you know all that stuff?" Justin asked.

"Why, from library books," Grandma said. "When I knew I was coming, I read up on the things I'd be seeing." She laughed. "You didn't think I was that smart, did you?"

We all laughed. In fact, we were still laughing when we drove into our lane. Naturally, Grandma took one look at the large, pink brick house and said *Wonderful!*

Mom, forgetting all thoughts of fatigue, gave Grandma a tour of every room. *("Wonderful!")*

With Grandma finally settled for some rest in the "guest room," (which is really Dad's study with a hideaway bed), we realized there was about an hour until supper time.

I can't speak for Grandma or the rest of the family, but personally, I collapsed on my canopy bed.

Chapter 3

First Choice
Saturday Night

Lord, it's me, Jennifer.

"What is it?" Justin poked the food Dad had just put on his plate from the large, oval casserole.

Mom smiled. "Justin thinks our meals are a foreign conspiracy," she explained to Grandma. "I never realized before how many recipes sound like they originated in other countries."

"Well?" Justin knew everybody was looking at him.

"It's turkey tetrazzini."

"I can't believe it," my brother said. "We haven't even had a turkey yet; how can we have leftovers?"

"Turkey is a country, Dummy. Like Italy," Pete said.

"They sell the parts separately," Mom explained.

"Why are you defending this delicious meal to a pee-wee kid?" Dad asked. He gave Justin a stern look.

Pete grinned. "See, Grandma, your wish is coming true. We're doing just what we always do. Watch the Greens in action!"

Grandma started to laugh. Things must seem funnier to her because she isn't in charge.

"Of course, we don't always eat in the dining room with candles," Pete explained.

"You weren't here last week," Justin said. "We did it with Matthew Harrington!"

I nearly died. The last person I wanted to discuss tonight was Matthew! I have been trying very hard all day to forget that he's taking somebody else to tonight's high-school basketball game.

"Matthew lives down the road," Mom said. "He happened to be here when the bird feeder came. He put it up for us and got us started identifying birds."

"Where did you put the feeder?" Grandma asked. "I didn't notice it."

"Right outside the family-room window," Mom said. "I'm really enjoying my early Christmas present!"

"I'm glad," Grandma said. She and Pops were the ones who gave it to us. Well, really to our mother.

"How long can you stay, Mom?" Dad asked. I was thankful he had changed the subject.

"A week," Grandma said. "I hope that isn't too long. I got a special super-saver rate for flying on weekends, but I have to stay seven days."

18

"I wish you could stay longer," I said. And everyone else agreed.

We spent most of the meal bringing Grandma up-to-date on what's been happening. Justin told about making the basketball team. Pete and Dad said they're learning to work the computer. And Mom told about going to her new neighborhood Bible study.

"Jennifer's turn," Dad said.

While the others were talking, I realized that a lot of what happens in my life is very *personal*. What I mean is, I could tell Grandma. But I hardly wanted to announce everything at the dinner table!

Luckily, I remembered the horse. "Somebody I know has an older sister who might sell her horse," I said.

"The one you borrowed?" Grandma remembered.

"Right," I said. I had told her about how I nearly fell off because I didn't fasten the saddle tight enough. "That's the one. But tomorrow you'll be able to see me ride Rocky! He's the horse I've taken my lessons on."

"Are we all going?" Justin asked.

"Yes," Mom said. "We'll meet Chris at the stables. And after we watch Jennifer ride, Chris is coming back here for supper."

"Yea!" said Pete. As You know, she's too old for him, since she's my age. But he likes her a lot anyway. Not as a girl friend, naturally!

"How are things with you, Mom?" Dad asked Grandma. "You've spent a lot of time catching up on our lives. Tell us about you."

"I just take life one day at a time," Grandma said. "Although it was good to be at Bob's, the time came when I had to go home and face the future."

"Did Uncle Bob fly down with you?" Pete asked.

Grandma nodded. "I don't think I could have walked into our condo alone that first day," she said. "Jay's memory was everywhere." Grandma's eyes filled with tears. "But Bob couldn't stay long. He really had to get back to the store."

I thought of Grandma all alone. I reached in my pocket for a Kleenex. I didn't have one, so I just sniffed.

"But then the church people started coming. And it was OK. They are wonderful. Our minister's wife stayed with me the night Bob left. After that I knew I could make it one day at a time."

"Are you keeping the fishing boat?" Pete asked.

"Certainly," Grandma said. "We'll need it for fishing! Your grandfather loved that boat," she added. Naturally, we all knew that already.

"I think you're wonderful!" Mom said.

"I have a wonderful Lord!" Grandma said. "He will never leave me or forsake me. It's really true," she smiled.

"Let's have a fire in the family room," Dad suggested. "The boys can help me."

"Sounds like the gals get to clean up the kitchen," Grandma teased.

"Sorry," Dad said. "We'll clean up the kitchen. You make the fire!"

20

"Serves me right," said Grandma. "Where's the wood?"

I wondered if we'd play Uno. We always played when Pops was alive. But maybe it would make Grandma feel bad. I thought of suggesting Monopoly.

But Grandma asked where we kept the Uno cards. "Pops wouldn't want us to miss out on the fun just because he's not here," Grandma said. So we sat at a table near the fire and played Uno. Just like we used to do. Well, almost like we used to do.

* * * * *

I was all set for bed when there was a light tapping at my door. I figured it was probably Justin. "Enter," I said.

"Pajama party?" Grandma asked.

"Well, sure," I smiled. "Come on in."

We sat on the bed. I am not supposed to sit on the bed. I forget why. But Mom would understand this time.

"Sorry I can't serve cocoa," I said, remembering our time together in Florida. Then I realized I probably could sneak down to the kitchen and make some. "Would you like some?" I asked.

"It would probably blow our cover," Grandma said softly. She grinned. "I thought maybe I've missed some recent development in the Harrington brothers romance! What's happening?"

"Grandma," I laughed. "You're like a teenager!"

"Well," she said, "appreciation for romance never

21

dies. I think older women must keep the soap operas going."

So, Lord, that's why I was sitting up in bed telling my grandmother all about the past couple of weeks. She's a great listener. She wanted to hear about everything. The hayride and moonlight with Matthew. The ball game and talk by firelight with Mack.

"The funny thing is, Grandma," I said, "I still like both of them just the way I did before. Only now I like them more because I know them better. But I still can't choose."

"You don't have to," Grandma said. "Things will sort themselves out in time."

"Do you really think so?"

"You can count on it, Jennifer. The biggest mistake kids make is to rush into romance. It's like pulling open the petals of a rose to force it to bloom faster."

"I like that," I said. Remind me to think more about it later, Lord.

"Well," Grandma said, "it was just an illustration."

"By the way," I said, "do you know what to do with a bad pimple?"

"Not really," she replied. "I haven't been watching any medical programs." She glanced at her watch. "I'd better sneak down to bed before someone catches me."

I grinned as I watched her tiptoe down the hall. Now there, Lord, is a *wonderful* woman!

I wish I had told her that!

Chapter 4

My Riding "Recital"

Lord, it's me, Jennifer.

Because Grandma wanted us to live our lives as usual, my brothers and I rode to Sunday school with the Harrington family. Our parents would bring Grandma afterwards, and we'd sit with them during church.

My pimple really hurt this morning. It's one of those large, painful bumps that I just know will last forever. Forget Rudolph. I look like a flashlight.

"Hi, everybody," Justin said, as we climbed into the station wagon. Matthew and Mack were both smiling at me! Start sorting, Lord! As for me, I just acted normal. You know, as cool as I could act with a large pimple on my nose. I sat next to Matthew. He was just acting normal too.

Mr. Williams teased us as we came into the junior-high department. "Well, if it isn't the Baldington brothers! And Jennifer Purple!" We smiled as we headed for our seats.

"Did your grandmother come?" Heidi Stoltzfus asked. She was wearing a baggy green dress. I tried not to pay too much attention to it.

"She sure did," I whispered.

"How long can she stay?"

Something seemed different about Heidi. I looked carefully at her face. She was smiling her huge smile, but her eyes looked red. Something was wrong. "Are you OK?"

She just kept smiling. She's been smiling a lot since the hayride.

Mr. Williams looked right at us. He had written "General Revelation" on the blackboard.

I tried to think of all the generals I had heard of. I couldn't remember one called Revelation.

"What does nature teach us about God?" Mr. Williams asked.

Kelly Robbins said, "God is artistic." Her father is our minister. Mr. Williams wrote *artistic* on the board.

Then Matthew said, "God is powerful." So, naturally, Mr. Williams wrote *powerful* on the board. I'm sure You get the idea.

I raised my hand. "God forgives," I said.

"How does nature show us that God forgives?" Mr. Williams asked me. I was embarrassed. I couldn't think

24

of a single way. "I guess it doesn't," I admitted. You know how I hate to seem stupid in Sunday school, Lord.

But Mr. Williams didn't want me to seem stupid either. "You're getting ahead of us, Jennifer," he smiled. "Does nature show God's sense of order?" he asked.

Well, naturally, it does! Sunrises, sunsets. Winter follows autumn, etc. I smiled too, and Mr. Williams wrote *sense of order* on the blackboard. He also wrote *creative,* and *cares about little details,* and *magnificent.*

"Now, how do we know God forgives?" Mr. Williams asked.

I raised my hand again. "Because the Bible tells us He does," I answered.

"So," Mr. Williams smiled, "nature alone isn't enough to tell us all about God. Is that right?" Everyone nodded. "How about the person who says he's going to worship God on a mountainside? Can he?"

"Sure," Kelly said. "But unless he knows what the Bible says, he won't know all he could about the God he's worshiping." Kelly was right. Her father must have told her. But Lord, I think it's really true!

When we went to our classes, I got to tell everyone that Grandma is here. Our teacher even prayed for her, which I felt was thoughtful.

We've been meeting Dad and Mom in the parking lot between services, and today it was really sort of cold outside. Heidi came with me because she wanted to meet Grandma. Also, the three oldest Harrington guys stopped to meet her. Grandma smiled. I was pretty sure she'd act cool, and she did. She was too smart to let on that it was a big deal.

Church was about the same as usual. Until just before our minister prayed. He told us then that Mrs. Williams was going to the hospital for tests. Frankly, I was very surprised. You too, Lord? When church was over, a lot of people crowded around the Williams family.

Dad did not want to join the group. "Let's go," he said. Grandma was treating us to dinner at a restaurant in King of Prussia, and he wanted to beat the crowd. As You know, we made it.

Grandma let us order whatever we wanted—just like Grandpa always did. I couldn't help remembering.

After dinner, it was back to our house to change our clothes. I put on my riding pants and boots. Everybody else changed into something "more comfortable." That means, among other things, that the guys took off their ties, and the women took off their good shoes. Grandma changed into designer jeans! I wonder if they're new?

To be honest, I'm not sure Dad was too thrilled about going right out to the stables. Our Sunday newspaper, which weighs several pounds, was sitting there in the family room. I think he was *tempted*. But Dad was a good sport. "OK, everybody. This is your big chance to see Jennifer Green, equestrian," he announced.

"What's an equestrian?" Justin asked.

"It has something to do with keeping your balance," Pete told him. "You know, not falling off." I couldn't tell if he was kidding or not.

26

Mom gave Dad directions to Twin Pines stable. Chris McKenna, my riding instructor, was standing outside waving as we arrived.

"Hi, Chris," Pete said.

I introduced Chris to Grandma, and Chris suggested we all go inside, where it's warmer.

While I got Rocky ready to ride, Chris told my family some things about horses. "Horses can learn new habits," she said, "but their personalities stay pretty much the same. When Jennifer comes out, you'll notice that Rocky is gentle. You don't need to be afraid. But you should never stand behind any horse!" she warned.

I could hear Chris talking to my family. I felt very proud when Rocky followed me out of the stall.

"Wow, he's big," Pete said.

"I agree," Dad said. "They look bigger up close."

While Chris talked, Justin paid no attention. I could see him looking carefully at Rocky. He eased around to where he was standing almost in back of the horse.

Chris also noticed Justin. As she explained the difference between Eastern and Western riding, she stepped back near him.

Suddenly, while Justin stood behind Rocky, right where she told him *not* to stand, Chris reached out her foot and kicked my brother!

Justin, who thought the horse had kicked him, jumped. Did You notice the look on his face? It was all I could do to keep from laughing out loud. Meanwhile, Chris just calmly kept explaining about Eastern riding.

27

"OK, Jennifer," Chris said. "You can take him into the ring and mount."

It was sort of like a piano recital. Without the piano. As Chris gave me directions, I showed my family all I had learned since I started lessons last summer. Every time I rode past, they all clapped. Well, naturally, Chris didn't! But everyone else did.

I felt very confident. Because I've learned to do things by *feel,* I was able to watch the expressions on people's faces. My brothers were impressed. At first, Mom acted nervous, but she perked out of it. Dad looked proud. And Grandma smiled from ear to ear.

"It's *wonderful,* Jennifer!" Grandma said.

Dad complimented Chris on her teaching. Naturally, that made Chris feel good. "I hear there's a horse for sale," he said. "Do you think you'd have time to take a look at it?"

Chris nodded. It was just what I had hoped he'd say.

Chapter 5

My Dream May Come True!

Lord, it's me, Jennifer.

I really had hoped I could take Chris to youth group with me so she could learn about You. But, to be honest, there just wasn't time. After I finished riding, I had to groom Rocky.

Pete tried to get Chris alone so he could talk to her. He is so obvious! But, instead of just telling him to bug off, she suggested a tour of the stables.

"I think, if you don't mind, I'll just watch Jennifer," Justin said. Naturally nobody minded.

"Be careful he doesn't kick you," my brother warned me.

"I'm careful," I said. "I always talk to him while I work so he isn't surprised."

"How can you talk to a horse?" Justin asked.

"The same way you talk to a person," I said.

"So," he said, "start talking."

Well, it's sort of like when someone sticks a tape recorder in front of you and suddenly you can't think of a word to say!

I started brushing Rocky's neck. I said stuff like, "Whoa, Boy. You did great today!"

"I can't believe it," Justin said.

"Dad was impressed, Rocky."

"Sure he was, Rocky," Justin said. "So impressed you might just get replaced by another horse! Maybe even one that doesn't kick people."

"Don't tell him that," I said. "He might feel bad."

"This is sickening," Justin said.

"Whoops," I said. I stood back, mostly out of the way.

"Yuck! That's really sickening," Justin said.

I had to watch where I walked. But I managed to do at least a fair job of wiping Rocky's coat with my grooming cloth.

"All set, Jennifer?" Chris asked.

"Phew!" said Pete.

"You don't know the half of it," Justin said. He rolled his eyes.

"I can guess," Pete said.

Chris and I sat in the back of the station wagon. Under the circumstances, it was the least I could do.

30

Grandma turned around in her seat. "If I didn't know better, I'd have guessed you've been riding all your life," Grandma told me.

"Well," I said modestly, "I'm not really all that good. But I have a great teacher."

"I thought you'd be older." Grandma smiled at Chris. "What grade are you in?"

"Eighth," Chris said. "Same as Jennifer. But I have been riding since I was a baby."

"Your parents must be proud of you," Grandma said.

"They sure are," Chris said. I didn't look at her. I couldn't believe it. As You know, her parents could care less! I suppose Chris doesn't admit that to just anyone. Does everyone have personal secrets, Lord?

While I showered, Chris played ping pong with Pete, Justin, and Dad. Being an only child, she enjoys being part of our bigger family. Personally, I can see real advantages to being the only one. But not if my mother got drunk and my father worked all the time. Like hers do.

I felt lots better when I got into clean underwear. I decided to wear my new cords for the first time. There wasn't time to wash my hair again, so I had to brush it and tie it back. No one would notice it anyway. They'd be staring at my pimple. Now it looked like a headlight!

"Did you really mean it about having Chris look at Ashlie's horse?" I asked Dad at supper.

Dad grinned. "Of course, I don't know anything about horses or riding, but it's pretty obvious that you enjoy it. Wouldn't you agree, Sue?"

31

Mom nodded. I think they had talked this over ahead of time. Am I right, Lord?

"At first I thought it was just something girls go through," Dad continued. "But you've stuck with your lessons long enough to satisfy me that the whole thing isn't just a fantasy."

"I can't believe it!" I said. The truth is, it *was* sort of a fantasy. But Chris is helping me make it come true. I looked at my friend. I wish I could do something to make her home life happier. Can You, Lord?

"I wouldn't know a good horse from a bad one." Dad looked at Chris. "Will you look at this horse Jennifer's talking about?"

Chris smiled. She likes Dad. I can tell. "I'd be honored," she said.

"Do you know about prices?" Dad asked.

"I know, in general," Chris answered. "I'll check it out with somebody to make sure."

"Don't get one that kicks!" Justin said.

"Hey, don't pull that," Chris told him. "I told you not to stand behind him."

Justin looked embarrassed. "You're right," he said. "A horse is an awesome animal. Can we ride him sometime, Jennifer?"

I was speechless. It never ever occurred to me that I'd have to share my dream. I zoomed from ecstasy to doom in five seconds flat!

"One thing at a time," Dad said.

Grandma has this way of diverting potential disaster.

"Jennifer told me you have won a lot of ribbons," she smiled at Chris. "I'm sorry to be so ignorant, but how did you get them?"

"At horse shows," Chris explained. "You can enter different categories and compete with others at your level."

"Is that what goes on in Devon?" Mom asked.

"That's one of the biggest shows in the country. You just missed it this year. It's held the end of May and beginning of June," Chris explained. "It lasts more than a week."

"Where's Devon?" Pete asked.

"It's that place with the big board fence, Dummy," Justin said.

"I find your attitude condescending," Pete replied.

"Enough!" said Mom.

Everyone looked at Pete. "I'm improving myself," he said. "I try to learn a new word every day."

"Actually," Chris said, "Devon is the name of a town."

"When did you start?" Justin asked Pete. "I haven't noticed anything different before!"

Well, as You know, it was another of our normal dinner-table free-for-alls. Chris seemed kind of amazed. Grandma, of course, is getting used to us.

After supper, everybody helped clear the table and load the dishwasher. I think it was Chris' first time to see the inside of a dishwasher. That's because McKenna's have a cook named Nellie. But Chris faked it by watching how the rest of us did it. Mom's system, naturally.

"Are we going to play a game?" I asked.

"Let's take a fifteen-minute break and then meet for Uno," Mom said. "OK?"

"Want to go to my room?" I asked Chris.

"Sure."

When I closed the door, I twirled around. "I'm so happy I could explode. My own horse!" I said.

"One thing at a time," Chris grinned.

"You already know Ashlie's horse, don't you?"

"Sure. But *buying* him is different."

"How are things at home?" I asked. "Any better?"

"She kept Dad and me up almost all night," Chris said. "I can't take too much of that."

"Why doesn't your father *do* something?"

"What can he do? He tries hiding the liquor, but she always gets some anyhow," Chris said.

"There must be something he can do," I said. Is there, Lord?

"Sometimes I feel like running away," Chris said. She put her lips together in a straight line.

"Where would you go?" I asked.

"There's got to be somewhere," Chris said.

Although she had never played Uno before, Chris was good at it. It was fun to see her relax and get into the family fun. But when the door chime rang announcing her ride home, I thought she changed. Nobody else seemed to notice. Did You?

"May I hug you, dear?" Grandma said. Chris seemed to like it.

"May I?" Pete asked. Naturally everybody laughed.

I waved to the chauffeur, and he waved to me. Then they were gone.

"Homework?" Mom asked. We all looked blank. But she was right. We'd have to go back to school in the morning.

Just before I got in bed, I sneaked down to Grandma's room. "I don't want to give away any secrets," I said, "but Chris has a tough time at home. Her mom gets drunk a lot."

"Poor dear," Grandma said.

"I'm worried about her," I admitted. "I thought maybe if I took her to youth group she'd learn about God. Do you think that would help?"

"Of course that could help," Grandma said. "But don't you think she could learn about Him here too?"

"I guess I didn't think of that," I admitted.

Back in my room I thought about it some more. Lord, however You do it, it's OK. But please help her! And, by the way, thanks about the horse!

Chapter 6

Megan's Plans

Lord, it's me, Jennifer.

Sorry I didn't have time to read my devotional book this morning. You know I could hardly go to the Winter Carnival committee meeting with dirty hair! Not with Megan's eye on Matthew!

I decided if I pretend the pimple isn't there, other people may not notice. The truth is, I look like a lighthouse. All I need is a foghorn.

When I got downstairs, not only was Grandma up, she had already eaten a poached egg!

"Do you have plans for the day?" I asked.

"Sure do," she said, smiling at Mom. "What time did you say the boys' bus goes?"

"You sound pretty anxious," I said. Not that I blame her. Although I think Friday is my favorite day of the week, Mom's is probably Monday. No offense, Lord. Naturally most of us like Sunday also!

I headed for the bus stop. It had been a super weekend.

"Hi, Jennifer," Stephanie said. Lindsay just stood there.

"Stephanie!" I replied. "You're just the person I want to see. My dad said we can consider buying Ashlie's horse."

"Excellent!" she said. "Ash is getting a car for graduation."

"Wow," I replied. That would ease the pain of giving up her horse! "Dad wants a friend to look King over. He doesn't know much about horses."

"Whatever," Stephanie said. "Let me know when."

"Did you ride this weekend?" I asked them. Lindsay and Stephanie always stick together. Their horses are even stabled together.

"We were out all day Saturday," Lindsay said. She still hasn't told me her parents are splitting, so I'm still pretending I don't know. "Here comes your boyfriend."

The Harrington brothers arrived together just as the bus came.

"Winter Carnival committee meeting today?" I asked Matthew. He's always been the one to remind me.

"Uh huh," he said smiling. "I'll meet you at your locker."

As usual, I saved a seat for Heidi Stoltzfus.

"I love your grandma," she said when she got on the bus. "She doesn't look like a grandmother!"

"What is that supposed to mean?"

"I guess I thought all grandmas looked like mine—plump and older," she said. "But they come in all shapes and sizes," she smiled.

"Just like other people," I laughed. "You look different."

"Do I?" she grinned. "I was wondering when you'd notice."

"I noticed yesterday," I admitted. "But I couldn't figure out what had changed."

"That's funny, Jennifer. I thought everybody would know right away."

I tried to figure it out. "Oh, no!" I said. "You got contacts!"

"Friday afternoon," Heidi said. "Yesterday my eyes watered so much I thought people would think I was crying."

"You look great!" I said. Her eyes were hardly red.

"My doctor said I can only leave them in a few hours at a time. But by the end of the week I should be all set."

Lord, what a change! I can hardly believe it.

"We prayed for Mrs. Williams at youth group," she said. "Missed you, by the way."

"Did Mack announce the next social?"

"Yes, and it sounds great, Jennifer. He told everyone how nice your parents were to invite us to have it at your house. I can hardly wait."

"It should be fun," I said. "I hope it's as good as the hayride."

It was a normal Monday. I have to write another theme for language arts. There's going to be a test in social studies. And You wouldn't believe the homework in math!

At lunch I sat with Heidi. Stephanie and Lindsay don't sit with me because of Heidi. They don't like her because she isn't cool. She's asked me to help her with her clothes, but we haven't had time.

"Have you ever thought of having your ears pierced?" Heidi asked.

"Sure," I said. "But not recently. Why?"

"I just wondered. Would you like to go and do it together?"

I nearly choked. "I'll think about it." Which, as You know, means *I'll have to ask my parents!* "Where were you thinking of having it done?"

"The mall in King of Prussia. That's where Kelly went."

"How much does it cost?" I asked.

"It's free," she said. "Of course, you have to buy some earrings. I thought maybe we could do it when we go shopping."

"I'll think about it," I said again.

After my last class I put my books in my locker and looked for Matthew. He was nowhere in sight. I couldn't decide whether to keep waiting or walk toward Room 204. Finally, I started walking.

40

"Where's Matthew?" Megan said. Not "Hi, Jennifer."

"I don't know," I said. At least he hadn't gone without me!

"It's funny, but he never mentioned he wasn't coming," Megan said. She made it sound as if he told her everything. "Let's wait a few minutes more." She took out a brush and fluffed up her hair.

The two guys in the room looked bored. I noticed the seventh grader roll his eyes like Justin does sometimes. The eighth grader grinned. Megan wasn't watching. She had her eye on the door Matthew would enter.

My first impression of Megan had been correct. She is beautiful. She could do television commercials for bouncy hair shampoo. Or toothpaste. Or diet-cola. Or, *(it pains me even to think it!)*, a clear skin cream.

"If we aren't having a meeting, I'm leaving," one guy said.

Reluctantly, Megan began. "The ticket committee wants us to build a snowman, since they're using snowmen on the posters," she announced.

"I thought we were having a mascot in a snowman costume," I said.

"Too small," Megan said. "We need a really huge snowman on the stage when the Winter Carnival king and queen are crowned. You know, something that will make a real statement!"

Well, we decided to build a really huge snowman. Not out of snow, of course. Although *that* would be easier! It would have a chicken-wire base filled with crepe paper flowers. Sort of like a float for a parade. Naturally, it was Megan's idea.

"Won't it take lots of crepe paper?" the seventh grader asked. "And who'll stick it in?"

"The committee will," Megan said. "We can do it at my house."

I wished Matthew were there. He would know if the plan would work. And he'd be brave enough to oppose Megan if it wouldn't. On second thought, I'm not so sure about that last part!

As You know, Matthew sure acted dopey around Megan last week. Did he take her to the basketball game when I couldn't go with him? I can hardly stand the thought! I don't mind him taking someone else. Not too much. But not Megan! She is obviously after him, but Matthew can't see it.

"Well?" Megan was looking at me. "Will you get the crepe paper?"

"I guess so," I said.

"Then it's all set," she said.

The guys said they had to go and hurried out. They were probably afraid she'd remember that nobody was getting the chicken wire.

"Next week I'm petitioning for *queen,*" Megan told me. Probably because I was the only one still in the room.

"How does it work?" I asked. Being new at this school, I've never even been to a Winter Carnival. Megan's in ninth grade, so it's her third one. "You have to get fifteen people to sign your petition. Then they put your name on the ballot," she explained. "The whole junior high votes. The winners are kept secret until the carnival Saturday night."

"I suppose the king is chosen the same way?" I asked.

"Fast learner," she said.

I sat alone on the bus. Certainly there's no danger of *my* being voted *queen*. I hardly know enough people even to sign my petition!

On the other hand, Matthew's chances at *king* have to be excellent. He's one of the most popular guys in the school.

I came up with a fantasy for the future. Megan would be queen. Matthew would be king. They'd become an item. Perhaps eventually he'd get tired of her. And maybe then I'd have a chance.

Is this Your way of sorting things out, Lord? As I walked up our lane, I rubbed my tender nose with my mitten. It feels awful.

Chapter 7

Nothing Ever Happens

Lord, it's me, Jennifer.

Has it ever occurred to You how many *details* it takes to fill up a perfectly ordinary day?

When I first walked in the door, the house was so quiet I thought nobody was there. I hung up my jacket, stuck my books on the stairs, and went into the kitchen. Something smelled good.

"We're in here, Jennifer," Mom said. I followed the voice into the family room.

"It's wonderful," Grandma said. "We were watching the birds."

"Can I get you some hot coffee?" I took their cups into the kitchen. "Anything to eat?" I called.

"Grandma made cookies," Mom said.

"How was your day?" Grandma asked.

"OK," I said. "Same as usual."

"I thought maybe Matthew would come in with you," Mom said.

"So did I," Grandma grinned.

"He disappeared," I told her. "Never even came to the meeting. Do you think I should call Harringtons?"

Mom thought a minute. "I don't know. Maybe he'll call you."

"Is Pete over there?" I asked.

"I'm not sure," Mom said. "We got home from shopping a little late."

"What did you buy?"

"Mostly things for me," Grandma said. "Shopping in my town isn't the best. It was wonderful to get into a big department store again."

"Can I see?" I asked Grandma.

Grandma nodded as she finished her coffee. "Want to come, Sue?"

Mom shook her head. "Go ahead. I have to make a salad. The roast should be nearly done." She picked up the dishes.

Grandma had quite a few boxes and bags on the couch. She opened one.

"I love it!" I told her. The dress was blue, and the jacket was sort of blue and navy knit. "Can you really wear that in Florida?"

"It will be perfect," Grandma said. "I didn't realize

46

until I moved there that Florida has fashion seasons. We don't wear white accessories at all in the fall."

" "I didn't know that," I said.

"Most people don't," Grandma laughed. "They say that's how you can pick out the tourists."

"Were we *that* out of it?" I thought back to our visit.

"Of course not," Grandma said. "It isn't important anyway."

"You always look so nice," I said.

"I try to wear what looks best on me," she said. "A woman helped me decide which colors are most becoming."

"Is that called *having your colors done?*" I asked.

"Same thing, I guess," Grandma said. "Why?"

"Mom talked about doing that. But I forgot to ask her how it turned out," I admitted.

"Do you think she looks different?"

"I think she does," I said. Frankly, I haven't thought about it too much. As You know. "How does it help?"

"People look and feel better when they wear styles and colors that look best on them," Grandma said. "Don't you have some things that make you feel terrific?"

"My pink sweater," I said immediately. "I could wear it every single day."

"Clothes like that are the real bargains—no matter what they cost," Grandma said. "Although you don't have to tell your father I said that."

I laughed, and she smiled. She really is beautiful. At least, that's my opinion.

47

"Have you ever bought something that was *in* and discovered you felt awful in it?"

"My two-piece bathing suit," I admitted. "I never told anyone that before. And my baggy sweats. I have a pair of clogs I thought I couldn't live without, but now I never wear them."

Grandma laughed. "Everybody makes a few mistakes along the way. Once I spent a small fortune on a camel-colored dress, which I wore *once*. It hung in my closet for years before I finally realized I was never going to wear it again! I even kept buying accessories for it. But there it hung!"

I laughed again. "I forgot to mention my cape! Justin thought I was Supergirl!"

Grandma opened a bag containing a navy leather purse. "I lucked out on this today," she said. "They were having a sale. Half off!"

"It's super," I said. "Wouldn't mind having one like that myself!"

"Want to go tomorrow?"

"I'd love to!"

"Let's check with your mom," Grandma said. "And, speaking of her, she probably could use some help now."

Grandma stirred the gravy. "That's a grandma's job," she insisted.

"Because nobody else knows how to make it anymore," Mom said. "It's a lost art. Like pie crusts."

The front door opened, and Pete came straight back into the kitchen.

48

"Is Matthew OK?" I asked.

"Can't you even say 'hi'?"

"Sorry," I said. I realized I did the same thing Megan had done. "How was your day?"

"Same as usual," he said. "I've got a hug for Grandma!"

"Ummmmm," she said. "I like that!"

"How about me?" Mom said.

"Maybe when I'm old enough to hug girls," he grinned. "By the way, Matthew just got home."

Just after he said it, the phone rang. I made a grab for it. Naturally, no one else was even trying anyhow. You probably noticed. My family did too.

"Green residence. Jennifer speaking," I said. Very cool. I tried to ignore my family's giggles.

"It's Matthew," he said.

"What happened?"

"No big deal. I fell in gym and had to go and get X rays. I didn't have any way to let you know."

"Are you OK?"

"Just a sprained ankle," he said. "How was the meeting?"

I was starting to tell him about it when my father and Justin came home. "I have to eat," I said. "Can you call me back later?"

"Poor Matthew," I told my family after our dinner time prayer. "He has a sprained ankle."

"How'd he do it?" Justin asked.

"I'm not sure," I said.

Justin lost interest. "Now this," he said, "is what I call a real dinner! Good old meat and potatoes."

"Red, white, and blue American," Mom said.

"It looks brown and white to me," Justin said. "Except for the carrots."

The phone rang again. "No calls during dinner," Dad said.

"It might be important," Mom said. "You never know."

"If it's important, they'll call back."

So we all sat there and listened while the telephone rang thirteen times!

"Tell us about your day, Peter," Grandma said.

"It was OK," Dad said. "About the same as usual."

"Didn't anything happen?" I asked.

"I hired a new sales rep." He spooned gravy over his pot roast.

"Male or female?" Pete asked.

"It happens to be a woman," Dad said.

I cheered, and Pete and Justin booed. I couldn't tell if Grandma or Mom were voting. Could You, Lord?

When Justin started smarting off, Dad gave him a *look*.

"He doesn't want to be a male sheboyganist," Pete explained.

Dad smiled. "And how was *your* day?" he asked Mom.

Chapter 8

Another Phone Call

Lord, it's me, Jennifer.

Frankly, I'm really amazed that You can keep everybody and everything straight. You know, we don't have that big a family, but Dad thinks we need a switchboard. Our telephone situation in the evenings is crazy.

During tonight's meal, the phone never rang again. "See," Dad said. "It couldn't have been important."

Well, he was wrong! I'm on pots and pans this week. So naturally we have this big roasting pan with stuck-on gravy. I was trying to get it clean when the call came. Dad answered in the study. "It's for you, Jennifer," he called.

I dried my hands and expected to tell Matthew about Megan's huge snowman. But it was Kelly. "I'm calling for the Sunday-school prayer chain," she told me. "Are you there, Jennifer?"

"What's wrong?" I asked. We never have a prayer chain call unless there is something *big* to pray about.

"It's Mrs. Williams," Kelly said. I sat down and waited. "You know she had tests today at the hospital. Well, they found out she has something called lymphoma."

"Is it serious?" I asked. I've heard adults ask that question.

"Very," Kelly said.

"Will she need an operation?" I asked.

"No. She'll be coming home tomorrow. But she'll have chemotherapy."

"What's that?" I asked.

"It's when you go into the hospital and they give you powerful medicine to kill the germs. And Mom says it can make you sick."

"Then what's the point?" I asked.

"The point is that if she doesn't have the treatments, the disease can be fatal."

I got that awful feeling back in my stomach. "She could die?" I asked.

"It's a kind of cancer," Kelly explained.

That I've heard of! "But she isn't old," I protested.

"There are all kinds of cancer, Jennifer. Sometimes even kids get it." She paused. "Sometimes God heals people. That's why everybody is praying—to ask Him to make her better."

"Well," I said, "I'll pray right away. Am I supposed to call somebody else?"

"Heidi Stoltzfus," Kelly said. "Do you have her number?"

"I do," I said. "Kelly, are you scared?"

"Sort of," she admitted. "I'll talk to you later."

I hung up the phone and sat down again. I closed my eyes. "Lord, please help Mrs. Williams.... And Mr. Williams.... And the kids.... Thank You that they are Christians.... And please make the medicine more powerful than the germs.... Amen." As You know, that was all I could think of to say. Then I had to call Heidi right away.

Well, that Heidi has to be the nicest girl in Pennsylvania. She is so sweet. "Every single person is different in God's plan," she told me. "We can count on Him to be loving and gentle and faithful."

"Are you sure?" I asked.

"What I think doesn't matter," she told me. "But we can trust what it says in the Bible!"

"Thank you, Heidi. See you tomorrow."

The funny thing was that I didn't cry. I mean, wouldn't You think that I'd fall apart? Instead, I felt OK. Incredibly peaceful, even. I couldn't believe it.

The next call *was* Matthew. He wondered if I had heard the news. "I prayed already," I told him. "But why don't I feel like crying? I cried like a baby when Grandpa got sick."

"Emotions are hard to figure out, aren't they? When I

first heard about it, I cried. But now I feel better. Do you feel like telling me about the committee meeting?"

"Might as well," I said. I tried to explain about the snowman.

"I don't know how we can shape the chicken wire," Matthew said. "But I'll think about it. Hey, my brother needs the phone."

"Thanks for calling back, Matthew," I said. "Hope your ankle's OK."

"Bye."

"Good-bye." I hung up. The dish water was only luke-warm, but I attacked the roasting pan with a scouring pad.

The thing is, the rest of my family really doesn't *know* the Williams family. Which makes a difference. Suddenly, I realized that *I* don't know them like most of the other kids do! But I still care a lot, and my family does too. When I went in to tell them about Mrs. Williams, Dad suggested we make a circle and pray together, which I thought was nice.

Since we kids had homework, we couldn't play Uno. To be honest, Dad brought home a briefcase of work from the office. Grandma seemed to enjoy sitting alone in the living room with a paperback mystery she brought from home.

And Mom went out! She said she'd be back in an hour or so, but she didn't say where she was going. Speaking of mysteries!

I was so busy studying, I heard the garage door go

54

back up before I even took a break. Then I heard Mom and Grandma talking and laughing. Does Grandma know where Mom goes on Monday nights, Lord?

I showered and put on a robe before I went downstairs. I looked Mom over carefully. She *does* look prettier!

"Would you still like to shop tomorrow?" Grandma asked.

"It seems kind of gross to think of bargains when Mrs. Williams is so sick," I said. "Is it? Like, gross?"

"Life does go on," Grandma said. I guess she ought to know.

"We've been thinking, Jennifer," Mom said. "Would you like to see a color consultant? I think you'd like the gal I went to."

"Could I, Mom?" And suddenly I had a far-out idea. "Do you think Heidi could go with me? I've promised to help her with getting her wardrobe together. And, frankly, I don't know where to start!"

"The girl I met Sunday morning?" Grandma asked.

"You've got it," I said. "Heidi Stoltzfus. She never even had a pair of jeans until the hayride!"

"What a nice idea, Jennifer," Grandma said. "I could take them over, Sue."

"How much does it cost?" I asked.

Before Mom could answer, Grandma spoke up. "My treat," she said. "For both girls." I couldn't believe it. Grandma added, "One of the nicest things about having extra money is being able to give happiness to others. In fact, that makes *me* happy, you know!"

"But will Heidi and her parents understand?" I asked.

"You let me take care of that," Grandma said confidently. "Now what is her number?" She left and went into the kitchen.

I just looked at Mom and grinned. Boy, was Heidi going to be surprised! "How about an appointment?"

"You let *me* take care of that," Mom said confidently. "Is tomorrow after school OK for you?"

I nodded. "I hope Heidi's free," I said. Mom went into the kitchen to join Grandma. I just waited—and hoped.

"All set!" Grandma and Mom were both grinning.

"What shall I wear?" I asked.

"How about that pink sweater?" Grandma suggested.

I couldn't think of a better idea myself.

Chapter 9

Cathy's Magic

Lord, it's me, Jennifer.

Grandma was waiting for us in Mom's car after school. "I'm so excited," she said, as Heidi and I got into the back seat.

"We're the ones who are excited," I said.

"It was hard to concentrate during classes," Heidi admitted.

"Did you ever do this with Aunt Elizabeth?" I asked. "She's Grandma's only daughter," I told Heidi. Naturally, You already know that!

Grandma laughed. "Well, hardly," she said. "I don't think color consulting was state-of-the-art in those years. And, anyhow, Elizabeth wouldn't have been interested."

"Was she a hippy?" I wondered.

"Not really," Grandma explained. "But all the young people then just wore old jeans all the time. And none of the girls fussed over their hair like my generation did."

"Did you get uptight?" I wondered. It was hard to imagine Grandma being uptight.

"I sure did sometimes! It was hard raising young people. We finally learned to forget about clothes and concentrate on more important issues—like drugs and sex."

I glanced at Heidi. She looked embarrassed. "Where are we going?" I asked Grandma. Just then she pulled up in front of a red brick house.

"Cathy?" Grandma said to the woman who came to the door, "I'm Mary Green. This is Sue's daughter, Jennifer. And Jennifer's friend, Heidi Stoltzfus."

"Hi," Cathy said. "Come on in." She was younger than I thought she'd be. "This is Jeffrey," she said. He was lying in a playpen in the center of the living room.

Cathy hung our coats in a small closet. "I'm glad you could come while there's still daylight," she said. "Colors change under artificial light."

We left Jeffrey and followed Cathy back to a bright room with light walls and a huge mirror.

"Please sit down," Cathy told us. "I'm going to start by turning you into ghosts!" she laughed, as she draped white sheets around each of us. I felt like a mattress.

"I'm glad you're with me," I told Heidi. She nodded.

"The whole point of doing this is to find out which colors look *best* on each of you," Cathy said. "At first glance, people are quite similar. But we all have different

58

skin tones, eyes, and hair colors."

We watched Cathy bring over several boxes of solid colored fabrics—everything from black to a rainbow of pastels.

"Now, I'm going to try several colors on Jennifer. Try not to look at the cloth. Instead, look at Jennifer's face."

I felt stupid. I glanced at my pimple in the mirror. I hoped it wouldn't destroy the whole test!

"Which looks better—this (orange), or this (pink)?"

Well, frankly, I've always hated orange anyhow, so I couldn't see how this could lead anywhere! Naturally, the pink looked better!

"She looks prettier in the pink," Heidi said. Bravo!

"OK, now let's try the pink—and this." She held up camel color. "Well?" Cathy asked.

"Definitely the pink," Heidi said. I agreed. As a matter of fact, I looked sort of sick in the other one! I couldn't believe it.

"Now, how about this one?"

"She looks good in the blue too," Heidi said.

"Fine," said Cathy. "You're catching on! Now which blue is better, this one, or this?"

No contest! "The second one drowns me out," I said. Heidi nodded.

"Let's try black," Cathy said.

"Yuck!" I said. "I look like an orphan."

"That color makes some people look beautiful," Cathy reminded us. "But not Jennifer."

"Notice how pretty your eyes look with this purple?"

Incredible! I've never owned anything that color!

Well, Grandma just smiled as we discovered the magic of color.

At first Heidi acted shy. Is that why Cathy had me go first?

"I look bad in the orange too," Heidi said.

"Not *bad,*" Cathy said. "But not as good as something else."

Heidi grinned. "Bad," she said.

"OK. Bad." Cathy laughed. "How about this?" She draped Heidi in a soft pink."

"Wow!" I said. Heidi blushed. Suddenly, Cinderella had been touched by the fairy godmother!

"I'll bet that's your favorite color, isn't it?" she asked.

"I've never had anything in pink in my whole life," she said.

"Let's try blue," Cathy said. But that blue was too bright. The next one was wonderful.

I held my breath when Cathy draped Heidi in green— the same green she had worn Sunday. It looked just as bad today. "Not for you, Heidi," Cathy said. "But let's try this one." It was green also, but a different shade. It looked OK. "Now, this."

If I knew how, I'd probably have tried to whistle! Cathy smiled also. "Here, Jennifer," she said. "Pull her hair back for me." I stood up and gathered Heidi's curly hair into kind of a pony tail.

"You are beautiful," my grandma said softly.

Heidi smiled shyly. "I never was before," she said.

"Color is magic," Cathy said. And Heidi and I didn't need convincing.

Well, it turns out that Heidi and I look good in the same colors! Our hair and eyes aren't even the same, but I guess it has something to do with our skin tone.

Cathy told us that color isn't the only thing to consider when we choose clothes. She said we should consider our personalities, our figures, shape of face—stuff like that. "Notice how much better you look when your posture is good." We stood up straighter! And she was right!

"Hardly anyone can afford to go out and get a whole wardrobe at once," Cathy said. "But if you have a plan when you start out, you can add things that go with each other and with the best of what you already have."

"What happens with people who don't look good in blue? Like, how about jeans?" I asked.

Cathy laughed. "For you two it isn't a problem. Others wear them anyway, of course. But they look prettier with tops that flatter their faces."

We could hear the baby starting to fuss. "I'm going to put together a book of color samples that are best for each of you. Since I don't have time now, maybe you could get them tomorrow."

"I'll pick them up," Grandma said.

"When you girls go shopping, take your books with you to the store. Otherwise, it's impossible to remember the shades."

We walked into the living room. Jeffrey was glad to see his mother!

"Try to get one whole outfit that you feel good in," Cathy said. "Matching navy or burgundy shoes and purse would be good.

"And since you already have blue jeans, you might get a skirt and slacks in blue or gray. Your shirts and sweaters will be the softer, lighter colors. And everything will be coordinated. That means you can wear each top with every skirt or pants." She picked up the baby.

"And we won't even look at anything yellow or black!" Heidi said.

"Or orange!" I laughed. "How about plaid?"

"It's probably easiest to start with plain colors," Cathy told us. "But you might happen to find a patterned vest in your colors. You could wear it with any of the pants, skirts, and tops."

"You know," I said, as we put on our coats, "this could really be fun. Shopping, I mean."

"It is," Grandma smiled. "Sort of an adventure in finding your own best look. And you don't even have to try on the stuff that doesn't look good or fit into your plans." She reached for her checkbook.

"You can pay me tomorrow," Cathy said. "And I'll put my phone number with your color swatches," she told Heidi and me. "Let me know if you have any questions."

When we got into the car, Heidi was beaming a huge, happy smile. "The new me," she laughed. "I can hardly wait to surprise everybody."

"Well," Grandma said, "may I give you two a ride to

the mall to go shopping tomorrow after school?"

"Do you have other plans?" I asked Heidi. She shook her head.

"We might even let you come in the dressing room, Grandma," I told her.

"Let's not get carried away, Jennifer," she laughed. "I'm great at disappearing when I'm not needed."

The girl we dropped off at the Stoltzfus house looked a lot different from the one I met last summer. She sparkles already. I'm sure You've noticed too. Is it the contact lenses?

Chapter 10

A Happy Season

Lord, it's me, Jennifer.

I tossed my book bag on the floor next to my closet door. What the situation called for was organization. I would sort out all the clothes I already owned. All the pants first. Then the tops....

Someone was knocking at my door. "Enter," I said, without looking up from hanging a pair of tan cords. Yuck. How could I ever have bought them?

"Jennifer." It was Mom.

"Hi," I said. "Just taking a little inventory."

She didn't say anything. I stopped and turned around. "Hey," I said, "you're mad. What did I do?"

"Nothing," she said.

"So, what's the problem?" I felt uncomfortable.

"I don't suppose it ever occurred to you that I might like a little help," she said.

"Sorry. I'll be right down."

While I set the table, Mom perked out of it. "Let's just eat in the dining area tonight," she said. Our kitchen has this little part that's three steps down—sort of behind the sink. It's where we eat breakfast.

"Great," I said. "Which dishes?" Choices, choices.

All of a sudden I started noticing the colors of everything! Well, naturally, I've known colors since I was about two! But one set of place mats is an entirely different blue than another. And I realized how many different "whites" there are. Before, I always thought *white* was *white!*

"Heidi and I are both *summers,*" I told Mom. "What are you?"

"I'm a *winter,*" she said.

"So is Grandma. Did you know that?" I put a white plate on each rust place mat. "Where is she?" I asked.

"Resting. I think she's reading her book."

"What did you guys do today?"

"Brandywine River Museum, lunch, and Longwood Gardens," Mom said.

"No wonder you're tired."

"She loved it. And, of course, it's one of my favorite days."

"Sometime will you take me?" I asked.

"I didn't realize you'd be interested."

"Just because Pete and Justin groaned doesn't mean I'm immature," I said.

Mom smiled. For the first time. "You're OK," she said. "Sorry I got on your case."

"I guess I needed it," I admitted. She didn't disagree!

Suddenly, the place was alive with people and voices. I could hear Grandma asking my brothers each to choose a special place they'd like her to take them. And Dad was hugging Mom. And, somehow, everything was back to normal again. Did You help, Lord? I mean, does tension bug You? Just wondered!

At supper, I announced that Heidi and I are both *summers*.

"Does that mean you can't stand the cold weather?" Justin asked.

"Maybe Grandma could take you to Florida!" Pete said.

"I'm a *winter!*" Grandma laughed.

"Then you can stay here with us! You can have Jennifer's room!" Pete said.

"That isn't fair!" Justin said. "What am I?"

Mom, Grandma, and I all stopped eating and looked at him. "Does he have gray rings around his eyes?" Grandma asked. Well, it was too dark to tell.

"Maybe he's a *spring,*" Mom said. "That yellow sweater looks good on him."

"I can't believe it," Pete muttered.

"Neither can I," Dad agreed. "Aren't we going to eat before this gets cold?"

Mom laughed. Usually she's the one to say that!

After supper, I was very careful to help. In fact, I did more than my share. Did You notice?

Then the phone started ringing. Mostly it's for me. (Now that Nicole has stopped calling Justin, my brothers don't get many evening calls.)

Chris called to ask if I wanted to go along when she checked out King. "Felix can take me tomorrow, and Stephanie said it's OK. Do you want to come along?"

"I can't tomorrow," I said. "Are you disappointed?"

"Well, it's probably better if you don't come this time," she said.

"Why?" I asked.

"You might blow it." She can be very blunt. "At this point it's a business deal. You'd probably be emotional."

I think she's right. "But it's my best chance," I said.

"Your father didn't say you had to get this horse. If King's not right, there'll be other chances."

"Let me know," I said. She promised she would.

I just hung up when it rang again. "Green residence, Jennifer Green speaking," I said.

"Hi, it's Heidi," she said. "I called to thank your grandma for her help and encouragement. I'm really excited."

"Me too," I admitted.

"Mom said I could invite you, your mom, and your grandma to go with us to the big Farmers' Market in Lancaster County Saturday. We can have lunch with my grandma."

68

"It sounds neat, Heidi. But I'm not sure what time Grandma's leaving. Can you hang on while I get her?"

Grandma couldn't believe the call was for her! "It's Heidi," I told her. I didn't want her to think it was bad news or something.

Well, since I was standing right there, I could tell we couldn't make it Saturday. Grandma said her flight leaves early that morning. "But we'll see you after school tomorrow," she said. "Bye, dear!"

"You'll have to come again, Grandma," I said, hugging her.

"Of course I will," she said. "Hey, the week's not over yet!"

I grinned. She was still standing with me when the next call came. "Back to my book," she said. "It's really getting exciting."

It was Matthew. Grandma turned around in the doorway and silently cheered. She is so funny! Then she left.

"Good news about Mrs. Williams," he said. "She's coming home for a few days before her treatments begin." He told me his mother had visited her at the hospital. "Mom says she's incredible!" he reported.

I felt happy and relieved. "Have you ever known anybody who got better?" I asked him.

"Sure. Not from anything this serious. But I've read about people who have."

"How does praying help?" I asked.

"I'm not exactly sure," Matthew said. "But God wants us to pray for each other. And He says that sometimes we don't get answers because we *don't* pray."

"I just wondered," I said.

"I talked to Megan today," he said.

Oh, no! "So?"

"I told her we'd have to find another way to make the snowman. She said you're getting crepe paper."

"I didn't get it," I said.

"That's good. I was afraid that's where you were this afternoon. I looked for you."

"My grandmother took Heidi and me somewhere," I said.

"Are you having a good time?"

"We sure are," I said. "The time's going fast. She's leaving Saturday morning."

"Hey," said Matthew. "Will you go to the basketball game with me that night?"

"Sounds good!" I said. "Of course, I'll have to check with my parents. Can you wait a sec?"

"On my way back to the phone to accept, I motioned to Grandma. She acted like a teenager!

Chapter 11

Shopping Spree

Lord, it's me, Jennifer.

Did You realize that today was absolutely the first time in my entire life that I've gone shopping by myself? In other words, without my mother! I sort of figured she'd give me a lot of advice at breakfast. Wrong!

"Your grandmother said to tell you she'll pick up your color books from Cathy before she meets you after school," Mom said.

I wish I were a better actress. I didn't want Mom to feel left out. But, I didn't want her to think that I needed her either. And, all the time I was hoping she wouldn't be there with motherly advice. That's a lot of emotion to get into four words! "Are you coming along?" I asked.

71

"Thanks for the invitation," she said. "I still have to do my Bible study for tomorrow. Besides, you don't really need me."

Lord, maybe I'll audition for the next school play! Did You help?

"Jennifer, you didn't get a lot of new clothes before school started," Mom reminded me, "so your dad and I have decided to give you a clothing allowance!" When she told me how much I could spend and handed me a charge card, I nearly fainted.

"Wow! That's a lot of money!"

"Wait until you see the prices," Mom warned. "Remember, that's for everything—shoes, a coat, the works. Not just jeans!"

"Thanks," I said. Then I hugged her.

"You don't have to spend it all today," she said. I guess that really *was* advice, wasn't it? Oh, well.

I could hardly wait for the school bus to get to Heidi's stop.

She was excited too. "I'm glad we had our colors done," she said. "I've never really been shopping alone before. Now I won't feel so stupid."

Well, I'm glad too! Frankly, I don't know how I could have helped her otherwise! "I sorted out the clothes in my closet," I said.

"Me too!" She produced a sheet of paper. It was divided into types of clothing, colors, things that fit, school clothes, Sunday-school clothes—well, You get the idea! And I thought *I* was organized!

72

"I don't think you'll need much help. You've really thought this through!"

"Well," she laughed, "at least most of my things that are in wrong colors don't fit anyway! I hope the thrift shop needs lots of stuff for *autumns* and *winters!*"

"What does your mom think of all this?" I was sort of scared to ask.

"She's planning to make an appointment with Cathy next week!"

"I can't believe it!"

"She said sewing is too much work to waste the time making things that aren't flattering anyhow!" Heidi explained.

"How does she feel about your buying things?" I wondered.

"I think she's relieved! Of course, she'll still make some things—but I get to buy the material and patterns. Luckily, I've been saving my baby-sitting money for ages."

At lunch we stopped talking about shopping. I wondered if she knew any more about Mrs. Williams.

"She has such a positive attitude," Heidi said. "Very *up!*"

"I don't know her very well," I said. "I mean, I know who she is, of course. I think she's beautiful. And the Williams kids are so sharp. How are they doing?"

"Great," Heidi said. "Mom took over a casserole last night. They believe the Lord is going to make their mom well."

"What if He doesn't?" I said. "Won't they crash?"

"God gives people help when they need it," Heidi said. "Isn't this salad good?"

I agreed. "Did I tell you that I might get a horse?" I asked.

"You must be excited!"

"You know," I said, "I am. But, to be honest, it doesn't seem as important to me as it used to. I can't figure it out."

"That's interesting," Heidi said. "I wonder why that is?"

"When I find out, I'll let you know," I said. I laughed.

"Please do!" Heidi laughed too.

We carried our trays to the cart. What a great friend she's turning out to be. I wonder why I used to think she wasn't pretty?

* * * * *

"It's on sale!" I said. "It's the cheapest vest we've seen all afternoon."

"But it's not one of your colors," Heidi pointed out. "And it won't look good with the pants."

"Hey," I laughed. "Who is helping who? Or is it *whom?*"

"I'm just telling you what Cathy said."

"I know," I kidded. "Do you have to be such a fast learner?"

"What's next?" Heidi wondered. We each had our

74

arms so full that a nice woman had given us shopping bags.

"How about those shirts?" We walked over. I pulled out my book of color swatches. "Don't you think this looks OK?"

But Heidi surprised me by looking inside. "It isn't well made," she said. "See how crooked the stitching is? And these seams will pull out the first time it's washed."

We were having an excellent time. At first we both felt funny in the dressing rooms.

"What do you think?" I asked, trying not to act too embarrassed. "Shall we go in together?" When she didn't say anything, I told her that, naturally, we could find spots next to each other.

"But how could you see how I look?"

"I want your opinion too," I said. "Maybe we could meet in the hall?"

"Like on the count of three!" she giggled.

"It does seem kind of dumb," I said. "Hey, I'm willing if you are!"

"What's there to lose? Just our self-respect!"

I started to laugh. "I promise I won't like you any less!"

"Same here!"

So we went in together, pulled shut the curtain, laid down our purses, and hung up our possible purchases. Eventually there was nothing else to do. Except take off our clothes.

There is nothing in the world more revealing than a

75

dressing room. (Unless it's a gym shower!) And anyone who thinks all the girls are alike doesn't know anything! The way clothes can disguise our differences is almost a miracle! No offense, Lord!

What I had to realize is that nobody is perfect! And if Heidi could accept me in my present state, I could accept her back.

It got easier. And we really were able to help each other a lot—putting things back on hangers, running out to get an item in a smaller (or larger) size. Stuff like that.

"I just realized what it must be like to have a sister," I said.

"We *are* sisters, Jennifer. We both have the same heavenly Father!"

I guess You knew that all the time. Right?

"We have to meet Grandma in ten minutes," I said, looking at my watch. "Do we have time to look at those sweaters?"

"You know, Jennifer, I just thought of something. They have sweaters at the coat outlet. Maybe we should wait and check it out. I need a warm coat anyhow. What do you think?"

"What's an outlet?" I asked. All I could think of was a place where you plug in a lamp.

"It's a store where they sell things cheaper than in the department stores. There are a lot of them in Pennsylvania," Heidi explained.

"How can we get there?" I asked.

We looked at each other and smiled. Then we said, in

unison, "There has to be a way!" I say that a lot, and Heidi's started saying it also.

"Well," said Grandma, "looks like you did OK!"

"I'm pooped," I admitted. I used to think only old ladies said that. But Grandma looked like she could go forever!

"Did you see the purses on sale?" Grandma wondered.

"No. Where are they?"

"I thought you were pooped," Grandma said.

"Just got a second wind!" I said. "It happens that I need a purse. How about you, Heidi?"

"Let's go," she said.

Well, by the time we dropped her off, I was even more tired than the day we went sightseeing.

"Thanks," Heidi said, squeezing my hand.

Lord, thank You. For my new "sister!"

Chapter 12

More Saturday Plans

Lord, it's me, Jennifer.

It's gone! I was looking in the mirror at my hair, and suddenly I discovered that my pimple had disappeared. Was that a miracle? Anyhow, thanks!

As for my hair, it is a disaster! Since I had it cut last spring, it has grown out totally straight. And straggly. I bought a magazine to check out hairstyles. I discovered mine is the *queen of the jungle* look. Frankly, if I looked like most of the models, I think Dad would send me to Africa!

Anyhow, my blow drying takes so long now that I don't have time in the morning to read in my devotion book. Well, as You know, I glance at a verse. But somehow I don't think it's quite the same. Do You?

Today I observed Mom even more carefully. She is beginning to look absolutely cool. "Tell me about your hair," I said. "In five minutes or less." I finished my orange juice and started on the cereal.

"I go every week to the shop Chris' mother recommended. I get it cut once a month and a perm every three months," Mom said. "Am I getting ripped off?"

"Not at all," I said. "It looks excellent."

"Glad you approve," she said.

"I thought perms made you look electrocuted."

"Some do."

"I've been thinking of getting my hair styled," I said.

"Really!"

"Well, just thinking about it," I said. "You know, now that I've had my colors done and stuff."

"I like your scarf," she said.

"Thanks. Saw it in a magazine." I carried my dishes to the sink on the way out. "See ya."

At the bus stop Stephanie told me Chris had been to her stable to look at her sister's horse. "Will you keep King there?" she asked.

"I haven't thought about it," I admitted. "Why?"

"Just wondered. How *do* you pick your friends?"

"What's that supposed to mean?" I was getting mad.

"Seems like you'd rather be with Heidi Stoltzfus," Lindsay said.

"Or even Chris McKenna," Stephanie said. She gave Lindsay a knowing look.

"Hey, knock it off," I told them. "*You* were the ones who said I had to choose. Heidi and Chris already happened to be my friends."

"Just a little tip," Lindsay added. "That scarf looks dumb."

I couldn't believe it. It looked good in the magazine. Mom thought it looked nice. But what do we know?

"Hi!" Heidi said. "What's wrong?"

"Nothing," I lied. I was trying to untie the scarf without Stephanie and Lindsay seeing me.

"You can tell me!" she said. "What are sisters for?"

I changed the subject. "Are you wearing something new?"

"I was tempted," she smiled. "But I decided to wait until Saturday night."

"What's Saturday night?" I asked.

"I'm going to the high-school basketball game." Heidi grinned. "With Mack Harrington. He called last night."

"Great!" I said. I hoped my enthusiasm hid my surprise. "Guess what? I'm going with Matthew."

"Have you decided what you'll wear?" she asked.

"No. Have you?" I couldn't believe I was discussing clothes with Heidi.

"What about the pink sweater?" I could tell she would follow my advice. "Do you think we'll go together?"

"It would be fun," I said. And, Lord, I almost meant it!

Just as I finished hanging up my jacket, Mack stopped by my locker. "Hi, Jennifer!"

81

"Where have you guys been? I've missed you at the bus stop." It's the truth!

"Mom's been driving us in the morning because of Matthew's ankle. But it's nearly better."

I decided we'd both be less embarrassed if I told him I knew about Saturday night. "Heidi says she's going with you to the basketball game."

"You mean Saturday." He grinned. "Matthew and I decided it would be fun to all go together."

"Super," I said.

"I've got another practice game this afternoon. Want to come?"

"I can't today." Just last week I secretly vowed never to miss one! "We have a special Winter Carnival committee meeting."

"That's what Matthew said." We were walking into our homeroom. "Heidi's coming to watch."

Hmmm. Really. Funny she didn't mention it, Lord.

At lunch Heidi and I were back to clothes talk. "Have you thought any more about getting your ears pierced?" she wondered.

"Not really," I said. It was the truth. I can only deal with so much at a time. And right now my computer is overloaded.

"I'll wait for you," Heidi said. "It would be more fun to do it together. Besides," she grinned, "I'm scared."

I grinned too. "Same here." I did not add that I still don't have my parents' permission.

"Do you think Cathy had you hold my hair back

82

because she thought I'd look better with it shorter?" she asked.

I couldn't believe it! "I really don't know," I said. "Why don't you call and ask her?"

"Maybe I will."

Just then Stephanie and Lindsay rushed past our table.

"Hi, Jennifer," Stephanie said. I felt my face getting hot. I know they noticed I had taken off my scarf. They ignored Heidi altogether.

"They make me so mad!" I said.

"Don't waste your anger on people like that," Heidi advised. "It just encourages them!"

"You don't always have to be so nice," I said. Frankly, Lord, it gets a little sickening sometimes!

"I've known them a long time, Jennifer. I've had lots of time to learn to handle kids that get their fun out of putting others down."

As we took our trays to the cart, I wondered if Heidi had any friends before I moved here. Did she, Lord? Besides You, I mean.

Frankly, watching Mack Harrington's basketball practice would have been more fun than the Winter Carnival committee meeting. Even if Matthew *was* there.

"We certainly haven't much time," Megan said. "My idea was to get this snowman thing done this week. After all, the carnival is only a week away."

"A week is plenty of time if we don't have to mess with all those crepe paper flowers," Matthew said. "Styrofoam cutouts don't take forever."

"Can we do it Saturday at my house?" Megan asked.

Matthew looked at the rest of us. The other guys nodded. Grandma would be gone, and I could skip a riding lesson. I nodded too.

"Great!" Megan seemed pleased. Matthew would get the styrofoam. Megan would make the pattern. The rest of us would bring scarf, hat, pipe, etc. "Anything we forgot?"

"Knives," Matthew said. "Everybody bring a sharp pocket knife."

The other guys left quickly. Megan smiled sweetly at Matthew. "I feel so good about this," she said. "You've saved our lives! And don't forget *king* and *queen* petitioning starts tomorrow."

"I didn't know that," I said.

"Didn't you?" Megan replied. Then she smiled again at Matthew. "Yours can be the first signature on mine if you let mine be first on yours!"

Matthew stood there like a jerk. "I hadn't even thought about running," he said.

"Don't be silly," Megan said. "No one else would have a chance."

"See you Saturday," I said. My voice echoed in the room.

"Right," said Megan. But she was looking at Matthew.

Chapter 13

Grandma Catches Up

Lord, it's me, Jennifer.

"Hi! Anybody home?" I yelled.

"I'm watching the birds," Mom said from the family room.

I hung up my jacket, stuck my book bag on the stairs, and went down to join her. "Did Grandma go to see Justin play basketball?" It was their special time alone.

"Yes, and she's taking him out for pizza afterwards," Mom said. "Tomorrow is Pete's turn."

"Did you go to the neighborhood Bible study?" I asked.

"I had to. I was still the question-asker," Mom said.

"So," I said. "How was it?"

"Interesting," Mom said. "Do you know why the fishermen just walked off from their work to follow Jesus?"

"I'm not positive," I said. "There must have been something special about Him. What did the other women think?"

"Oh, He was special, all right! The voice from Heaven when He was baptized. Angels taking care of Him in the desert. And healing people! But how did the fishermen know that?"

"I'm not sure," I admitted.

"Of course, when the word got around about Him, everybody knew then. He couldn't get a moment's peace. Everyone was looking for Him!"

"Sounds like you learned a lot," I said.

"I did! But I still can't figure out how those fishermen knew."

"Who's the question-asker next week?" I asked.

"Betsy Porterfield," Mom said. "She hardly cried at all today."

"Well, it sounds like progress," I said. "Shall I set the table?"

"Frankly, I was thinking of trying Reuben's for hamburgers," she replied.

After we had eaten, I was in my room studying when I heard Grandma and Justin come in. They were laughing. Speaking of special, Grandma really is, Lord. Special, I mean. I waited a while to give her some time alone. After my shower, I planned to sneak down to see her. But the tapping on my door announced that she beat me to it.

"So, what's happening?" she asked.

I told her everything. I even told her I felt sorta jealous that Heidi's going with Mack! "I know it's stupid," I said.

She just grinned.

"Grandma, you're a riot," I said. "Maybe you should just stick around to see how it all ends!"

"No, I'll find out how it ends," she said. "But I can't stay here that long!"

"What will you do for fun when you get home?" I teased.

"There are always books and TV," she laughed. "Although real life is more interesting."

"Tell me something, Grandma. Do real-life brothers and sisters get jealous of each other?"

"You're kidding!" Then she saw I wasn't. "What causes jealousy?" she asked me.

I tried to remember how I had explained it to Justin last summer, but I couldn't. So I tried to think it through again. "Not being satisfied with what you've got?"

"Go on," she encouraged.

I tried to think. "Two people both wanting the same thing."

"Yes." She waited.

"One wanting what the other has."

"Good, Jennifer. Usually there's *pride* involved."

"Isn't it OK to be proud?"

"God wants us to feel good about ourselves," Grandma explained. "But when the Bible talks about *pride* it means we shouldn't always be comparing ourselves with somebody else—or what they have. *That* kind of pride leads to jealousy."

"How can you stop it?" I asked.

"By realizing God doesn't approve. Then you can ask Him to help you be more loving."

"It doesn't sound hard," I said. "But I've tried. And I know it isn't easy."

"The Lord is a good teacher, Jennifer. He'll keep giving you chances to learn as long as you need them." Grandma laughed. "And, just when you think you've learned your lessons, He'll slip in an opportunity for practice."

"Don't go home," I said. "You could teach me so much!"

Grandma hugged me. "I love you, Jennifer. The Lord will teach you. And we'll be together again soon."

"It's too bad I had to go to school this week!"

"Oh, no!" she said. "Look at everything that's happening! Besides, this is the most time I've ever had alone with your mother. We've had some lovely conversations."

"No kidding?"

"No kidding. I've got to let you get to bed, Dear," she said.

"I really do love Heidi. And I am happy for her," I said. "Most of the time."

"I know you are. Now, can you accept her as an equal—not just somebody you can help?"

"Sometimes it's easier to help," I said. "It makes you feel good."

"Good? Or better?"

"Thanks, Grandma," I said. "Do you think Matthew and Mack ever get jealous of each other?"

"Do birds fly?" Grandma laughed. She slipped out the door.

Lord, please forgive me! Thanks for sending Grandma. And keep those lessons coming. I bet You would anyhow, wouldn't You? By the way, do You ever laugh?

The next morning I asked Mom if I could get my hair styled at the place she goes to.

"I don't see why not," she said. "Justin wants to too."

"Justin!" I said. I can't believe it. "Are you going to let him?"

"Why not?"

Well, personally, I could think of a bunch of reasons. But I kept my big mouth shut for once.

"When are you free?" Mom asked. "He has basketball practice nearly every afternoon."

"You mean we have to go at the same time?" I asked.

"It's far enough that I'd rather not make two trips."

"Saturday afternoon?" I suggested. "After the snowman's done?"

"Shall I try for four-o'clock?"

"Can I have the stylist who does yours?"

"It's a man," Mom said.

"So?" I didn't want her to know I was surprised.

Just as I was putting on my jacket, Grandma came in. "Hi! Sleep well?"

I nodded. "I see you've stopped getting up so early!"

She and Mom both laughed. "I had my egg an hour ago," she reported.

"Big day?" I asked.

"We're heading up to Bucks County," Mom said.

"And after school Pete and I are doing our thing," Grandma said. She didn't say what their thing was. Frankly, I can't even guess. "We're having supper at Reuben's. What's Reuben's?"

"Hamburgers," I told her.

"That figures," she laughed. "Uno tonight? Or do you have a date?"

"Uno tonight!" I waved as I left for the bus.

Chapter 14

Our Secret

Lord, it's me, Jennifer.

Well, I noticed them right away. Mack and Matthew looked almost as if they were waiting for me. If they were jealous of each other, I certainly couldn't see it. Could You?

"Good morning!"

"Hi, Mack," I said.

"Did you hear the news?" Matthew asked.

"What news?" I couldn't think of any. Justin's getting his hair styled—or even my own—hardly fell into that category. At least for somebody else.

"Mrs. Williams is home!" Mack said.

"Mom's taking us over for a few minutes when she

drops off something for their supper. Want to come with us?" Matthew asked.

"Well, sure," I said. "If it's OK with everyone."

"We'll pick you up about five," Mack said.

I felt really super when I got on the bus. My homework was all done. I understand the math. Grandma's visit has been great. Heidi and I are "sisters" again. And Mrs. Williams is home!

During homeroom, Mr. Hoppert stood in front to tell us about petitioning for Winter Carnival king and queen.

"Petitions must have fifteen signatures," he said. "Those candidates submitted will be checked for scholastic eligibility. For a name to be placed on the ballot, a candidate must have a 3.5 grade average."

"How many petitions can we sign?" Eric asked.

"As many as you like." Mr. Hoppert smiled. "But, when it comes to actually voting, each person can vote only once for king and once for queen."

"How do we know if somebody has good enough grades?" Susan wondered.

"Don't worry about it for the petitions," Mr. Hoppert said. "The faculty will check scholastic eligibility before names are placed on the ballot."

"Don't the ninth graders always get it anyway?" Scott was a fatalist.

"It doesn't have to be that way," Mr. Hoppert said. "You can't win if you don't try."

"Any other questions?" There weren't. "Petitions may be picked up in the school office. They're due back by

92

Monday afternoon. Voting will be held during homeroom Wednesday."

I wondered if anyone from our room would try. I glanced at Stephanie, then at Lindsay. I couldn't tell a thing. Could You?

I'm not exactly sure when I got the idea. Maybe it started on the bus. Heidi was so excited about Mrs. Williams being home that she sort of glowed. Although she still hasn't worn any of her new clothes, I really thought she looked pretty. Do You agree?

Well, anyhow, I decided it couldn't hurt anything if I picked up a petition for Heidi. My thought was that if not enough people signed it, she wouldn't even have to know about it. Well, that's what I was thinking when I slipped into the school office. Nobody saw me.

At lunchtime, there was lots of excitement in the hall. Megan and her friends were cornering everybody they could find. I didn't even see Matthew.

"I'll sign your petition, Jennifer," Eric Franks said. He sits in front of me in homeroom and some of my classes.

"It isn't really mine," I explained. "It's for a friend."

"Whatever," Eric said. His was the first signature I got. I needed only fourteen more. Thirteen more after I signed it myself.

Stephanie and Lindsay had the nerve to ask Heidi and me to sign their petitions in the lunchroom. I had Heidi's hidden in my notebook.

"Do you think an eighth grader has a chance?" I asked Heidi.

"I don't know," she said. "Never thought much about it."

"*You'd* make a great *queen!*" I told her.

She just laughed. "Have you decided what to wear tomorrow night?"

Well, we talked that over while we ate our lunch. It really was lots of fun to have someone to talk to about going to the game.

"Mack played *super* yesterday," Heidi said.

"I forgot you went," I said.

"There was hardly anyone watching," she told me. "Maybe sometime we can all go to see the junior-high team game."

"Why not?" I said.

"If Matthew could go, we could all do something afterwards," I said. "Wouldn't that be fun?"

When I sat down in front of Mack, I turned around. He looked surprised. Naturally. I don't do that very often. As You know. I slipped Heidi's petition out and handed it to Mack. "It's a surprise. Want to sign it?"

Mack grinned. I think he likes surprises. "Looks as if we need a few more signatures. How about my taking it to basketball practice? I know the guys would sign it."

"You don't think she'll be mad, do you?" I asked.

"Heidi mad? You've got to be kidding! She never gets mad."

"Personally, I think she'd make an excellent Winter Carnival queen," I said.

"I do too," Mack said. "You'd be good too, Jennifer,

94

but not many people at school know you yet."

Well, that settled that. I knew it all the time anyway. "You won't tell, will you?"

"How about Matthew?"

"Maybe it would be better if he didn't know," I said. "Let's surprise them both!" I was trying to think fast.

"Awesome!" he whispered. As I told You, I think he likes surprises.

After school I took the regular bus home. So did Matthew. It was our first time alone together since he took someone else to last week's game.

"I'm excited about going tomorrow night," I told him.

"So am I!"

"Who won last week?"

"We did," he replied. "Mark was high-point man!" He's the oldest of the Harrington brothers. A senior!

"Is he going to college next year?"

"Sure," Matthew said. "Lots of schools have been recruiting him."

"What's that?"

"Trying to get him to come to a certain school to be on its basketball team. Of course, he's good in baseball too."

"Do you ever feel jealous?"

"Sometimes I'm tempted!" he laughed.

I laughed too. To be honest, I was sort of faking it. I don't understand the difference between being jealous and being tempted. Is there one, Lord?

"Where does Megan live?" I asked. "Maybe Mom can take us to the meeting."

"You can come with us," Matthew said. "I have all that styrofoam in the back of our wagon. Maybe Mark will drive."

"Grandma's leaving early in the morning," I said.

"Have you had a good week? She certainly is a lovely person."

"Can I tell her you said that?" I laughed. "She'd be thrilled."

"Why not? I meant every word."

"I wish you could have met my grandfather," I said. "He was very special also."

"He must have been," Matthew said. We stopped in front of my house. "Hey, I'll see you in a little while," he remembered. "I almost forgot about going to see Mrs. Williams!"

"I'll be ready," I said. I didn't tell him that I almost forgot also!

Chapter 15

We Visit Mrs. Williams

Lord, it's me, Jennifer.

As You know, I'm not very close to Mrs. Williams. For sure, she has to be a good sport. Does Mr. Williams tease his family as much as he kids around in our Sunday-school department?

I can tell from things he's said that he still thinks she's the greatest thing since cream cheese. I hope, if I get married, my husband still feels that way about me when we are older.

Not that they're old like Grandma and Pops, of course. But Jamie Williams is in eleventh grade, so they have to be pretty old. Brian's in seventh. And Erin is four, if You can believe that! Anyhow, that tells You something!

Well, to get back to my point, the only time I've ever spent with Mrs. Williams was on our junior-high retreat. She was in charge of sleeping in the girls' tent. That might not sound like much to be in charge of, but that's really all she had to do.

Naturally, I didn't realize then that she was going to be getting cancer! She probably didn't either. But I was so busy getting to know the other kids (and *the ropes*) that I didn't observe her carefully.

About all I can remember is that she laughed a lot. She didn't yell at us. During the day, she wore nice-fitting jeans, and at night she wore flannel pajamas and mens' black socks.

Did I mention her hair? Rachael Williams has dreamy hair! It has to be naturally curly—dark brown, thick, and bouncy. Come to think of it, I wonder where *she* gets it cut?

Matthew, Mack, and I were pretty quiet during the short ride over to the Williams home. Mrs. Harrington drove and talked. Her casserole smelled delicious! I think it's the same kind she brought my family after we came home from our grandfather's funeral. Lots of chicken in it. Not all noodles like some casseroles I've eaten.

"Your mom seems to be catching on well in the Bible study, Jennifer," Mrs. Harrington said. "And she doesn't seem afraid to say what she thinks."

"I'm glad," I told her. I didn't mention that most of us Greens aren't afraid to say what we think. She's probably noticed.

Jamie Williams met us at the door. "Hi," she said. "This is so nice of you!"

"Jamie, have you met Jennifer Green yet?" Mrs. Harrington asked.

Jamie smiled. "Hi, Jennifer," she said. "I've been hearing good things about you."

"Oh oh," I laughed. "Anyhow, I'm glad to meet you."

"How's your mom?" Mack asked.

"She's awake. At least she was a few minutes ago. I'll just check to see if she's ready to see you." She excused herself and left.

"You can slip off your coats and put them on this chair," Mrs. Harrington said. She took hers off too. "We can't stay long, but it is warm in here."

Jamie came back. "All set," she said. We followed her up the stairs.

I'm not sure what I expected.

"Hi, Martha."

Mrs. Harrington went over to the bed and kissed her. "How's it going, Rachael?"

"Can't complain," Mrs. Williams said softly. Then she looked around at the rest of us. "What a surprise! How nice of you all to come!"

"Everybody's been praying for you," Matthew said.

"We sure have," Mack said.

Well, as You know, I couldn't think of a single thing to say. So I just stood there and looked at her.

"Hi, Jennifer! What a special surprise," Mrs. Williams said. "How is your family? And your grandmother?"

She remembered! I couldn't believe it. "We're doing great," I said. "And Grandma is here spending the week with us. It's her first time in Philadelphia."

"Wonderful!" Mrs. Williams said.

"That's what she always says," I told her.

"Sounds like I'd better get *with it,*" Mrs. Williams laughed. "How about *'super?'*"

Everyone laughed.

"I'll bet it's good to be home again," Mrs. Harrington said.

"It sure is. If I ever get tempted to think of time in the hospital as restful, I hope I remember how hectic it was. A vacation it isn't! I've never seen such a procession of nurses and doctors. If it wasn't one thing, it was another!"

"How are you feeling?" Mrs. Harrington asked.

"I'm so thankful to be here with my family and in my own bed," Mrs. Williams said. "And our meals are taken care of. There's nothing like a church family at a time like this!"

"How about Erin?" Matthew asked.

"She goes to preschool in the morning, and her friends from Sunday school take turns having her over in the afternoon."

"I'm afraid we're tiring you," Mrs. Harrington said. "Anything you want us to tell everybody?"

"Tell them 'Thanks!' And to just keep praying for God's will," she answered. "I can tell you're praying. The Lord is so near! And I have such peace!" she said. "The doctors thought at first I was faking it, but I'm not!"

"Would you like us to pray now, Mrs. Williams?" Matthew asked.

"Please do." She closed her eyes. So naturally, I did too.

"Thanks, God, for Mrs. Williams and her faithfulness," he said. Then he just waited.

"Thanks for her family. Be close to them," said Mack.

"Give the doctors wisdom as they plan her treatments," said Mrs. Harrington.

The pause probably wasn't as long as it seemed. Finally, I said, "Thank You, Lord, for showing me that beauty comes from inside a person!" I hoped that wasn't too dumb. But it's just exactly what popped into my head.

"Lord, thank You that my times are in Your hands. Bless my dear family and my dear church family. Amen."

I opened my eyes and looked at her again. She was smiling. Her face was pale and looked tired. Her usually lovely hair was sort of stringy on the pillow. And I've never seen such a beautiful woman in my whole life!

Then Mrs. Harrington was saying good-bye, and we all joined in. "I'll call tomorrow, Rachael. Have Jamie let us know if you need anything."

"God bless you all!" Mrs. Williams said. "Keep praying!"

"We will. And we love you," said Mrs. Harrington.

I could feel tears coming to my eyes. I blinked several times and someone took my hand. It was Matthew.

Later, I was trying to describe the scene to Grandma.

"You can tell she's sick," I said. "But she really is beautiful!"

"I suppose," Grandma said, with a twinkle in her eye, "that her blanket and gown were in her colors!"

"I wasn't aware of any colors at all," I admitted. "Do you know what I mean?"

She took out her Bible and opened it. I listened while she read out loud, "'Your beauty should not come from outward adornment', such as braided hair and the wearing of gold jewelry and fine clothes. Instead, it should be that of your inner self, the unfading beauty of a gentle and quiet spirit, which is of great worth in God's sight. For this is the way the holy women of the past who put their hope in God used to make themselves beautiful.' That's from 1 Peter 3:3," Grandma said.

"That's exactly what Mrs. Williams is like," I said. "And you know what else? When Matthew took my hand, it felt so *comforting!* Not goose-bumpy at all. It's hard to explain. Do you know what I mean?"

Grandma did. So I'm sure You do too.

Chapter 16

Mom Tells
Her Secret

Lord, it's me, Jennifer.

Our whole family got up at the crack of dawn to take
Grandma to the airport. We sent her off with as many
hugs as when she came.

"I'll be back," she waved. "You come down when you
can!"

Everybody was unusually quiet when we got back in
the car. Of course, it was still pretty early for a Saturday
morning.

"How about a hoagie?" Dad asked.

"Yuck!" Justin muttered. Nobody disagreed.

"OK," Dad said, "we'll just head for home."

"It's hard to believe she's gone already," I said.

"The time did go fast," Mom agreed. "She's such a delightful houseguest."

"Where did you and Grandma go, Pete?" I asked.

"It's a secret," my brother answered. "If Mom can have secrets, so can I!"

"Good point," Dad said. "Where *have* you been going on Monday nights?" When Mom didn't answer, he asked if she minded if we all guessed.

"Go ahead," she said. "It might be fun."

"I think she's a spy for the CIA," Justin guessed. "Her cover is housewife and former room mother." He paused. "That's where she gets her foreign recipes. And her code name is I. Cook."

Everybody laughed.

"Personally, I think Mom's going to grad school," I said. "She's getting an MBA so she can start her own interior design business. And," I added, winking, "she has a crush on the accounting professor!"

"Wow!" said Justin. "What's the difference between the CIA and MBA?"

"MBA is a long-distance phone service," Pete explained. Mom just laughed.

"I think she's selling cosmetics," Pete guessed. "She sure looks pretty!" Mom grinned. Could he be right?

"Your turn, Dad," Justin said.

Dad, who had just been cut off by a huge semitrailor said, "You crummy so-and-so!" After a few minutes, when he got back to normal, he felt more like guessing. "Real estate school?"

104

Everyone, except Dad, of course, looked at Mom. She looked sort of embarrassed. "I guess I can tell you now. I've been going to Weight Watchers. I'm almost down to my goal."

"How come you never said anything?" Dad asked. "I had no idea you were even dieting!"

"There's nothing so boring as talking about dieting, unless it's hearing someone else talk about it," Mom said.

"I agree," said Justin. "Aren't the meetings Dullsville?" Honestly! As You know, he doesn't have a spare pound on him. He looks like a pencil stub with muscles.

"Who have you gone with?" Dad asked.

"I've gone alone," Mom said. "But I've met some very nice people there."

"And I thought you looked good because of your colors and haircut," I said.

"Everything helps," Mom said. "I really do feel better about myself."

Dad looked funny. Then he did a wolf whistle!

"Can you teach me how to do that?" Justin asked.

"Me too?" said Pete.

"If you have to be taught, you're too young to do it," Dad said. So, naturally, my brothers spent the rest of the ride trying!

As You know, I tried to mention that a woman's beauty isn't just *skin deep,* but nobody even paid any attention. I guess it just wasn't the right time.

"By the way," Mom smiled, as we pulled into our lane, "you all have given me some good ideas!"

When we got home, I cleaned my room. Also, I hope You noticed that I helped Mom strip Grandma's bed and start the laundry.

"I got you and Justin both hair appointments at four o'clock," Mom told me. "That way I can make just one trip. It was the latest they could take both of you. As a matter of fact, they had a cancellation. You were in luck."

"Hope we're done making the snowman by then," I said. "It's turning into a hectic day."

"What time's the game?"

I told her. "We're all going together," I said. "Heidi and Mack and Matthew and me."

"And I," Mom corrected automatically.

"Whatever," I said, just as automatically.

Mark, Matthew's older brother, drove us to Megan's. I saw that the back of the station wagon was full of styrofoam.

"Hi, Jennifer," Mark said, as Matthew held the door open for me.

"Hi, Mark."

"I hear it's snowman time!"

"Right," I said. "Mom can pick us up," I told them. "I have to leave by three-thirty."

"Can you come back for me?" Matthew asked Mark. "We have to get that snowman over to the school."

"How about next week, Old Buddy? The carnival isn't until Saturday night."

"Good point," Matthew said. "I will ride back with Jennifer."

106

Megan answered the door herself. I didn't see a parent anywhere. My parents wouldn't like that.

"Hi, Matthew," she said. "And Jennifer, too, I see."

We both said "hi." Just then the two seventh-grade boys on the committee were dropped off. They each carried a knife. I had forgotten mine!

"Where will we be working?" Matthew asked. His brother helped him carry the huge sheets of white styrofoam into a recreation room with green carpeting.

After Megan outlined the pattern, we started cutting. I had to borrow a knife from Megan's kitchen.

Have You ever cut styrofoam? I don't suppose so. Well, it must be made of millions of little pieces stuck together. And by the time we had cut for a little while, the whole room was full of little bouncing, white stuff. Like it was alive!

In the beginning, it was lots of fun. Well, actually, with all of us working, the carving didn't take long at all.

But cleaning up was murder! Matthew said it was static electricity—like when you walk on a rug and get "shocked." The whole carpet was alive with bouncing white balls. Since we weren't at my house, I could laugh. Even Megan laughed, and it was her house, so I didn't feel too guilty. Finally, we got most of it cleaned up.

"Something to drink?" Megan asked.

I said "I'd like a Pepsi, please." And everyone else agreed.

"By the way," Megan said, "I still have room for a few signatures on my petition for Carnival queen."

"Bring it in," Matthew said. "We'll all sign it. Right, gang?"

"How about *your* petition?" Megan asked Matthew.

"I don't have one," Matthew said.

"I can't believe it," Megan said. "Why not?"

"I'm just not into that this year," he told her.

It was the first I knew! I felt so glad that I even smiled when I signed Megan's petition. "Good luck!" I said. Which was sort of a lie.

"You'll help put it up, won't you?" Megan asked Matthew. "The snowman, that is."

"Certainly," he said. "Hope you don't mind keeping him here a few days."

"He should have a name," I said.

"We have to go," said the seventh-graders.

"Thanks for helping," Matthew told them.

"How about Oswald?" I suggested.

"Not Frosty?" Megan said.

"Too common," I said. Suddenly, I felt very bold.

"Oswald suits him," Matthew agreed.

We were all laughing when Mom drove up to pick me up. I reached for my jacket.

"Do you have to go?" Megan asked Matthew. "I was hoping you could stay. We never did figure out a time you could tutor me. Someone could take you home."

I looked at Matthew. Sweet, gullible, stupid Matthew. Lord, please don't let him get sucked into it!

"Not now," he said. "We can talk about it another time. Thanks for having us here today."

"Any time," she said. "Any time at all." It was the kind of thing that any other girl would have seen through immediately. The flirting, I mean.

"Gotta go," Matthew said. He even helped me into my jacket.

I felt so great I smiled right at her. "Yeah," I said, "thanks a lot!"

Guess I should thank You also! Consider Yourself thanked! A real lot.

Chapter 17

Cinderella Stoltzfus

Lord, it's me, Jennifer.

"Way to go!" Justin said, when he saw me at the front of the shop near the cash register. He tried to whistle, but nothing came out. Except air.

I grinned. I liked my hairstyle too. "You look cool too," I told him. "Why didn't I ever see you back there?"

"They have a special place for the men," he said.

"How come they let *you* in?"

"Bad joke. Very bad," he said. "They have two women who spend most of their time styling men's hair."

"A man cut mine," I laughed.

Justin let out a wolf whistle. "I did it!" he acted surprised. "Dad will be proud."

"Save it for other girls," I said. "Hey, I thought you were off women." He just got rid of Nicole Porterfield, Lindsay's sister.

"I am," Justin said. "But now that I can whistle, it won't hurt to keep in practice."

"I wish Mom would hurry."

"Basketball game with Matthew?" he asked.

"How did you know?"

"Pete told me. Sometimes he tells me stuff that goes on over at Harringtons." He glanced at me. "I hear Mark's going for a school scoring record."

"I didn't know that," I admitted. "I wonder if the whole family will be there?"

"Sounds like it," Justin said. "Pete's going with Mike. I sure would love to see Mark play."

"Are you hinting?" I asked. Justin grinned. "Sorry," I said. "Not with us."

"Well, it was worth a try," he said. "I like your hair anyhow!"

On the way home, Mom suggested that Justin could have Keever Stoltzfus over. He's Heidi's brother. And in Justin's class at school and Sunday school.

"I'll think about it," Justin said. "Do you think he'd be interested in going to the basketball game?"

*　*　*　*　*

Mom said I could shower first and eat supper in my robe. It was only hotdogs anyhow.

"I honestly think General Eisenhower managed to land

112

his troops on D-Day with less planning than this is taking," Dad said.

It seemed simple enough. Everybody was going to the same place—the high-school gym. But nobody wanted to ride with anybody else.

Of course, once Matthew can drive, we'll be all set! But that doesn't help now. With Mark on the basketball team, that meant he couldn't chauffeur.

Which left the parents. To be honest, having a parent drive isn't all that bad. They learn to become invisible and silent throughout this kind of trip.

But younger brothers are another story altogether! First Pete and Mike, then Justin and Keever—were all going to the basketball game. No offense, Lord, but it sounded like riding to Sunday school!

Pete was the one who told us how unhappy Matthew and Mack were. "Could *you* drive Mike and me, Dad?"

"The older boys don't want you along?" he asked.

"They don't!"

"I guess I can drive too," he offered.

"How about us?" Justin said. "Keever and I need a ride too."

Pete groaned. "Not them!"

I'm not sure how it all got worked out. Especially since everyone needed rides afterwards also. But I decided it really wasn't my problem. I needed all my emotional energy for getting dressed.

Heidi and I had decided, together, not to wear jeans. After all, we had both worn them on the hayride. And, besides, we both had new outfits.

If I do say so myself, I looked great! I wore a new blouse, corduroy pants, and a coordinating vest. The burgundy shoes and shoulder bag added just the right color accent.

When I looked into the mirror, I smiled. No more pimple. My skin looked clear. My hair looked glamorous, wavy and soft, with curls around my face. Matthew had never seen me look like this! I squirted the usual Charlie behind my ears. Ta daa!

Although I was all ready, I waited in my room until I heard the door chime. Then I could hear him greeting Mom. "Jennifer!" she called.

I opened my door and came down the stairs. I felt like I had never looked more beautiful in my entire life.

Matthew didn't whistle. It probably isn't considered cool. But after he watched me come down, he looked into my eyes and smiled. I wasn't exactly Miss Sobersides myself, You know. Actually, I can't remember either of us saying a single word. Did You notice if we did?

The next thing I knew, Matthew was telling Mom when he'd bring me home. The front door closed. And we were walking slowly toward the car.

"Your hair," he whispered, "is definitely prime time."

"I was hoping you'd like it."

When we got into the car, it *wasn't* like a ride to Sunday school. The Harrington parent was silent and invisible. I'm not even sure which one was driving!

"Hi, Jennifer," Mack said. He was friendly and warm.

114

Didn't sound jealous at all. "I really like your hair. It's different, isn't it?"

When Mack went up to Heidi's house to get her, Matthew reached over and touched my hair! Just lightly, not enough to mess it up or anything. There wasn't enough light for me to see his face. But when he took my hand, I didn't feel at all like I had yesterday! This was goose-bump time! Suddenly, I thought of Grandma and smiled even more. She'd understand!

And then, when Mack opened the car door, the light went on and I saw Heidi. I couldn't believe it!

"I got it cut yesterday," Heidi told us.

"You look great, Heidi!" Matthew said.

"That's what I told her," Mack grinned.

"You're lovely," I agreed. And I didn't feel jealous either. Not at all, as You know. She is my friend and my "sister." And I love her very much.

Somehow or other, we managed to get to the gym, and our driver disappeared. While the guys were taking our jackets to the coat-checking booth, I got to see Heidi in the bright light. Heidi's well-fitting slacks matched her purse and shoes. Her very first pink sweater was so sensational on her that her face glowed. And whoever styled her hair had done a magnificent job of taming her bushy, thick curls into a cap of ringlets.

"Do we know you?" Both Matthew and Mack were grinning from ear to ear as they approached us in the crowd. It was easy to see they felt proud of us.

"I'd like you to meet Cinderella Stoltzfus," I said, as I

squeezed her hand. She squeezed mine back.

"Aw, shucks," Mack said. "And I just checked a glass slipper!"

"You won't need it until midnight!" Heidi laughed.

"Right!" Matthew agreed. "On to the ball!" And he led me by the hand into the gym.

To the other kids, I probably didn't look *that* different. But Heidi was a sensation! Lots of kids, both from church and from school, said "hi" to the four of us.

We were having so much fun that it was hard to concentrate on the game. But, to be honest, the evening belonged to Mark Harrington. We yelled until we were hoarse every time he scored a point!

As You know, Mark did set a new scoring record for the high school! They even stopped the game to announce it. We four felt very proud of him.

Only once all night did I catch a glimpse of our assortment of younger brothers. I never did see Mr. and Mrs. Harrington. And, frankly, I hardly noticed the cheerleaders at all.

Afterwards, well, the Harrington station wagon might not have looked much like a royal carriage to You, but Cinderella and I didn't notice. And I don't think the handsome princes did either! We had such a ball at Reuben's, I'm sure nobody worried that the car might turn into a pumpkin drawn by white mice! Of course, to be honest, we were home by midnight anyhow!

I hope You find all of this as interesting as Grandma did!

Chapter 18

After the Ball Was Over

Lord, it's me, Jennifer.

The next morning, on the way to Sunday school, the Harrington station wagon was full of excitement.

"You'll be a hard act to follow!" Mack told his older brother. But he was smiling and proud. So was Matthew.

But the real hero worship came from Mike, Pete, and Justin. Especially Justin. "Can I have your autograph?"

"Sure," Mark laughed. He wrote his name on Justin's Sunday-school paper from last week. "Save it. It might become valuable, you know," he teased. Mark wore fame easily. "Don't ever forget," he reminded the younger guys, "that God isn't impressed with sports records! What He sees is what's in a person's heart!"

I remember Grandma saying almost the same thing.

Well, I guess Mr. Harrington thought we had enough heavy stuff. He started singing a song I can't remember ever hearing before. "H-A-double-R-I-G-A-N spells Harrigan." The ending was: "Harrigan, that's me!"

Then the whole family sang it faster. And at the end everyone almost yelled, "Harrington, that's me!" With little encouragement, even the Greens joined in. It was the most fun we've had on Sunday morning.

We arrived at the parking lot out of breath and with red faces. I felt super! Even before Matthew and Mark each took one of my hands to march me to the junior-high department.

"Hey," I laughed, "what about my stuff?" They carried it for me in their other hands.

It wasn't until we got inside that I remembered Mrs. Williams. The guys simmered down, gave me my purse and Bible, and we all walked with serious faces.

"Why so glum, chums?" Mr. Williams said. "I saw you last night, and I know things aren't that bad."

We grinned. Then we headed in to sit with our classes.

Heidi was already there. Everybody was telling her how great she looked in her new pale blue dress.

She handled it with surprising poise. She just said, "Thank you," and smiled. No fake humility. No pride that said she felt better than someone else.

As for Mr. Williams, he acted just like always. He teased the kids as they came in. I'm not sure what I was expecting, but this wasn't it.

118

"OK, gang," he said, "it's time to begin." We all were super quiet.

"I guess you've all heard by now that my wife, Rachael, has a kind of cancer. Well," he said, "this is where the rubber hits the road! Do we really believe what we've been studying every week? Or is it just words we read and recite?

"I've told you that God is good. Is that still true? I've told you that He loves me, that He gave me my wife and children. Does He still love my family?" He paused. Nobody even breathed.

"I've prayed with you for problems in your lives. Will I let you pray with me for problems in my own life? And do I still believe that God hears us?" The kids didn't make a sound.

"If anyone had told me a couple of weeks ago that cancer would hit my family, I wouldn't have believed it. You always think that's something that happens to someone else!

"And, if I *had* believed it, I would have been scared to death! Honestly. I would have said I couldn't possibly handle it!" No one moved.

"The Lord doesn't give you strength until you need it. But when you *do* need it, He is faithful!

"I can't possibly explain everything that's happening or what I'm feeling. But I can tell you, with all my heart, that I still believe in our loving, merciful, beautiful Lord Jesus!" The tears were streaming down his face now, and he was taking deep breaths. My eyes filled with tears.

Our class' teacher, Mrs. Spencer, stood up and went to the front. She put her hand on Mr. Williams' arm. "Bob, I'll lead the kids in prayer," she said.

It really was a prayer service, Lord. As You know. After Mrs. Spencer started things off, lots of the kids prayed. Since I tend to be emotional, I had to get out a Kleenex to dry my tears and blow my nose. But I could hear that I wasn't the only one!

As You know, I did not pray out loud. But You also know that I learned, once again, that faith in You is very real. Even in hard times, You are helping people. Maybe *especially* in hard times!

"Heavenly Father." It was Matthew's familiar voice. "We don't know Your will. But we all love You. And we love the Williams family. Please make Mrs. Williams well again."

"Thank You that You are real." That was Heidi. On and on we prayed, sometimes silently, until someone else spoke up. We didn't have time for our regular Sunday-school lesson, but Mrs. Spencer didn't seem concerned.

I honestly can't believe we spent that long just praying! Can You? The time went so fast. I wonder why I used to think praying was hard or boring? It's just talking to You, isn't it? And I do that all the time!

"Facts are easier to deal with than rumors," Mrs. Spencer told us when we finally went to our classes. "Mrs. Williams has a kind of cancer that can't be removed by surgery. The doctors have decided to start chemotheraphy next week. *Chemo* means drugs."

120

"Will she be able to stay at home?" Heidi asked.

"Yes, except for when she's having a treatment. That's done in the hospital."

"Is it painful?"

"I don't think so," Mrs. Spencer said. "But often patients become nauseated. You know, sick-to-their-stomachs. That's something we can pray about."

"My mother said her hair may fall out," Kelly told us.

"If that happens, she can get a wig," Mrs. Spencer said.

The first bell rang. "If we had known, we could have saved the hair from our haircuts," I told Heidi.

"I think she can do better," Mrs. Spencer laughed. "No offense!" We laughed too.

* * * * *

Just after my family finished eating, the phone rang. Pete answered. "Hi, Chris! How are you doing?"

I started toward the telephone.

"She wants to talk to Dad," Pete said. I couldn't believe it.

We all listened. "Hi, Chris. . . . Thanks. We all enjoyed Grandma too. . . . I see," Dad said. He looked serious. "I'm glad you checked it out. . . . No, I'll tell her about it."

I just knew it was bad news.

"I'm afraid you're going to be disappointed, Jennifer," Dad said.

121

"The horse?" I asked. "Someone else bought King?"

"No. Chris spotted a problem. She had a vet check him over yesterday. It's not really serious, but they don't think King's worth the price that Cantrells are asking."

"Well," I said, letting the news sink in.

My family just looked at me.

"Well," I said again. "I guess King just isn't the horse the Lord wants me to have!"

Everyone looked surprised. And I nearly fainted myself! Sometimes I even surprise myself. But not You, I'll bet.

"It really isn't the end of the world," I said. "On a scale of one to ten, it's only about a three!" Then, although I bravely tried to blink it away, a tear ran down my cheek. "Well," I admitted, "maybe a four!"

Chapter 19

The Ballots
Are Cast

Lord, it's me, Jennifer.

When I got to the bus stop, Matthew and Mack were already there. So were Stephanie and Lindsay.

"Am I late?" I asked.

"I think everyone else is early," Matthew replied.

"Anyhow, hi!" I said. It was practically dark outside. This week my hair has dried quicker, and I've had time to read in my devotional book.

"Wouldn't it be funny," Matthew said, "if we had real snow for the Winter Carnival?"

"This is the big week!" Stephanie told us. "Today's the day we vote for king and queen."

I had forgotten! "When do we have to fix the gym?" I asked Matthew.

"Not till Friday night. Old Oswald's all ready to go!"

"Who's Oswald?" Lindsay asked.

"Part of the decorations," I said. "You'll see."

As usual, I saved the seat next to me for Heidi. I thought everyone at school would be making a big deal about how super she looks. But nothing had changed. Stephanie and Lindsay still ignored her.

"Are we all going together to the Winter Carnival?" Heidi asked me.

"That's what Matthew said." I grinned. "You know, I've never been to one before. Are they fun?"

"I've never gone either, Jennifer," she said. "Last year I had to babysit Keever. I really didn't have anyone special to go with anyhow."

Wow, I thought. *Is she ever going to be surprised!*

In homeroom, Mr. Hoppert handed out the ballots. I glanced down the list of names. There weren't as many as I thought there'd be.

For *Carnival Queen:*
  Stephanie Cantrell
  BreAnna Diamond
  Megan Larue
  Heidi Stoltzfus
  Lynn Taylor

For *Carnival King:*
  B. J. Anderson
  Dunk (Harold) Boswell
  Brian Hagameier
  Forty-nine (Andrew) Simms

First, I glanced down the list of guys. Sure enough, Matthew's name wasn't there! And I didn't know a single one of the guys! What if I picked somebody awful? So I didn't vote at all.

I was so excited to see Heidi's name that it took me a minute to realize that Lindsay Porterfield's name was missing! Are her grades bad, Lord? Surely there would be fifteen people willing to sign her petition! How embarrassing! I honestly feel sorry for her! I can't believe it.

Naturally, I recognized Megan's name and Stephanie's. But I had absolutely no idea who the other girls were. I placed a firm *X* in front of *Heidi Stoltzfus,* folded my ballot, and had it ready when Mr. Hoppert picked them up.

On the way to our next class, I walked with Mack. "I hope she gets it!" I said. After all, she certainly qualifies for a "most improved" award!

"She just might have a chance," Mack said softly. "With three ninth graders on the ballot, it will split the vote."

"Who are the guys?" I asked.

"Ninth graders. All jocks except Brian."

"Who'd you vote for?" I asked.

"Heidi and Brian," he whispered. "It sure would be neat if somebody with *quality* won for a change!"

"Brian's nice?"

"Sure is. And Heidi's considered one of the friendliest girls in the school. Everybody likes her. Except the fast crowd."

At lunch I was waiting for Heidi when Stephanie and Lindsay made a point of stopping by. "Where's Little Goodie Two Shoes?" Stephanie asked. When I didn't answer, they left.

"Congratulations!" I said when Heidi sat down.

"Jennifer," she said, "do you know how my name got on that list?"

I felt my face getting hot. I had this terrible wave of guilt! I guess I should have asked her.

"I picked up the petition," I admitted. "I think you're the sweetest, friendliest girl in the school! And, now you're even the coolest! I hope you aren't mad at me!"

"Jennifer, you're a real friend," she told me. "Just how could I get mad at you?" She relaxed. "There's nothing at stake but my pride, I guess. But I sure was surprised to see my name!"

"Actually," I said, "Mack got most of the signatures. The whole basketball team, I think!"

Suddenly, the whole thing seemed so ridiculous that I started to giggle nervously. Then we both started to laugh. And it was hard to stop!

All during lunch, kids I've never even noticed before kept coming over to say "hi" to Heidi! And I had the feeling they could care less about her new clothes and haircut!

"Way to go!" Matthew said, after school. "I sure was surprised to see your name on the list."

"Tell me about it," Heidi said.

"Maybe we'll need a glass slipper after all," I said. "Of course, if you win, Mack won't have a partner!"

"For that long, I'll manage," Mack said. "First, she has to win."

* * * * *

126

It was late for the phone to be ringing. Mostly my calls come right after dinner.

There was a knock at my door. "It's for you," Mom said. "You can take it in the den."

"Jennifer!" It was Heidi. "Can you keep a secret?" Then she started laughing. "What a dumb question to ask *you!*" She kept laughing.

"What's going on?" I asked.

"I got it, Jennifer! A teacher just called me. I'm going to be Winter Carnival queen!"

"Yahooooo!" I yelled.

"Quiet, Jennifer! I'm not supposed to tell anyone."

"Who got it for *king?*" I asked.

"They didn't tell me. It's a secret, you know."

"Oh, wow! This is the greatest!" I said. "I can't believe it!"

"I'm supposed to change into a long, white dress in the teacher's lounge at nine-thirty Saturday night," she told me.

"Do you have a long, white dress?"

"Of course not!"

"What will you do?" I asked.

"Mom said she'll make me one. Can you help me pick out the material and a pattern tomorrow after school?"

"I'd be honored!" I said. And I meant it.

"You won't tell anyone? Not even Matthew or Mack?"

"Especially not Matthew or Mack!" I promised.

"Jennifer, I can't believe it! Do you think I'll wake up and find out I'm still Cinderella?" she asked.

"Not a chance," I assured her. "This isn't just a dream. This is real! Heidi," I said, "I just had a thought. Do you think it would be OK to tell Grandma? She'd be even more excited than we are!"

"Right!" Heidi said. "Oh, please call her. It would be so much fun for her. And tell her we'll send pictures later!"

"Super!" I said, very softly. "Otherwise, my lips are sealed."

"Jennifer, you're so funny! I love you, dear friend!"

"I love you too, Heidi. Good-night!"

* * * * *

My parents could tell I was excited. *Happy excited!* So, without needing to know the reason, they agreed that I could call Grandma from Dad's office. They explained how to do it. After I thanked them, they left and closed the door.

"Grandma," I said. "It's me, Jennifer! You'll never guess what's happened!"